Desdemona and the Deep

DESDEMONA
AND THE
DEEP

C. S. E. COONEY

A TOM DOHERTY ASSOCIATES BOOK

NEW YORK

DESDEMONA AND THE DEEP

Copyright © 2019 by C. S. E. Cooney

Cover art by Alyssa Winans
Cover design by Christine Foltzer

Edited by Ellen Datlow

A Tor.com Book
Published by Tom Doherty Associates
120 Broadway
New York, NY 10271

www.tor.com

Tor® is a registered trademark of
Macmillan Publishing Group, LLC.

ISBN 978-1-250-22982-3 (ebook)
ISBN 978-1-250-22983-0 (trade paperback)

First Edition: July 2019

For Julia, Moss & Desdemona

Desdemona and the Deep

1

A BENEFIT FOR THE FACTORY
GIRLS WITH PHOSSY JAW

FOUR STORIES ABOVE THE Grand Foyer of the Seafall
City Opera House, each painted panel in the barrel-
vaulted ceiling depicted a scene from one of the three
worlds. Which world it happened to be depended on
the tint and tone of the panel: daylight was for Athe,
the world of mortals; twilight represented the Valwode,
where the gentry dwelled; and midnight belonged to
Bana the Bone Kingdom, home to all the koboldkin.
Through these wheeling coffers of world-skies—day
dancing into dusk, dusk swirling into night, night into
day again—cavorted the bright-winged, the beautiful,
the bizarre. In that ceiling, at least, human and gentry and
goblin all intermingled together, like they had in olden
days before the doors between worlds were barred and
the boundaries set.

At the center of the ceiling, like the pistil of the three-
petaled World Flower, bristled a recently installed chan-

delier: an armillary sphere barbed with crystals, brass processes, and electric bulbs. It had been designed, ostensibly, to lull music lovers into a belief in a more orderly, benign, and attentive cosmos than evidence endorsed.

Standing precisely beneath it, a very short woman.

Her gown bore more rosettes and plumes than a parade float. The satin sash across her chest read: STRIKE THE MATCH. She had a round, rust-brown face, iron spirals of hair cropped close to her skull, and black eyes, lamp-bright. She wore on her brow a corona radiata of shining platinum. No mistake this woman had chosen for herself the spiked crown of heroes and deities; she wished to set an example for the gathered crowd. Heroes gave everything—and deities rewarded self-immolation with immortality.

"Good evening, friends and sisters!" Her voice was a one-woman brass section, as cheerful and relentless as reveille, complemented by the chime of her spoon against a champagne glass. "Good evening!"

Two hundred fifty-four women fell into an obedient hush. They rustled and ruched together at the foot of the Ceremonial Staircase.

"Let me begin," said the woman, "by thanking the Seafall City Opera House for so *generously* donating their Grand Foyer this evening. What a *beautiful* space for our *beautiful* cause!"

Her gloved palms initiated the applause, each muted thunderclap sweeping the room with a new flash flood of enthusiasm.

"Next," she continued, "but *no* less important . . . Let me thank *you* all so very much, my *dear* friends, for supporting our *first* annual Factory Girls with Phossy Jaw Charity Fund-raiser! So far, it has been a *wild* success!"

The answering applause lasted longer and was even more ebullient. The women, *her* women, had labored tirelessly, lobbied endlessly, and spent lavishly to make this night possible. Now, dressed in their finest, approved by their peers, buoyed by champagne and the glow of good work done well, they were prepared to commend themselves for it.

Against the back wall of the Grand Foyer, facing the Ceremonial Staircase, silent auction tables displayed their wares. As be-bannered, be-rosetted, and be-plumed as the mistress of ceremonies, they flaunted on fine linens the wealth of a queen's treasure house: basalt busts that bore the gravitas of deep antiquity, art jewelry from the museum collection, original paintings, travel vouchers, and baskets sporting rare vintages and costly cheeses sealed in red wax. Over all the tables presided a tall, youngish woman who bore little resemblance to the woman addressing the crowd, except perhaps in a certain stubbornness of jaw.

She watched her mother with an expression borrowed from her father's face—boredom, a hint of disdain, barely disguised exasperation. But something else flickered in her black eyes. An admiration so fierce it danced on the barbed wire wall between resentment and worship.

"How," asked a voice from behind her, "can it be an *annual* fund-raiser, if it's the first?"

The woman twitched a bare shoulder the exact shade of the bronze silk taffeta she wore. "Shut up, Chaz!"

"I was only asking," Chaz replied, affable and wounded.

"I am not speaking to you."

"You are though, Des," he argued. "You just *said*—"

"I am never speaking to you again." Lifting her chin but still not looking at him, Desdemona Mannering contradicted her dictum immediately. "You are *three hours* late, Charles Abelard Mallister. We had *plans*."

Mrs. Tracy Mannering—Mission Advancement Director for the Factory Girls with Phossy Jaw Charity, mistress of this evening's ceremonies, and Desdemona's mother—had personally assigned her daughter to oversee the silent auction tables that night. She had assumed that Desdemona would be delighted. So commanding, so inexorable, and manufactured of such titanium goodwill were Mrs. Mannering's assumptions that when Desdemona received her invitation to the benefit (along with a full duty roster), she had little choice but to agree to work the tables.

But if Desdemona knew one thing, it was this: if misery loves company, malice *adores* it. Aping her mother's style, she informed her best friend that he, too, would be dishing out auction items by the silver platterful at her mother's "Phossy Gals Follies," as she put it. What's more, she'd added with a burst of inspiration, he would be doing it en travesti, in a gown of his choice.

It would not be the first time Chaz had attended an event costumed like a woman. He occasionally wore gowns out to nightclubs, quite often to private parties, and always whenever spending an evening alone with Desdemona. But so far he had never worn one of his gowns to any function coordinated by the hoity-toity aunties of high society. Whether this was out of shyness or dread Desdemona could not tell, and had never asked, but she thought it high time Chaz outshone them at their own game.

When he'd protested, she'd simply scoffed. Those clucks, she'd said, wouldn't care if Chaz showed up "in the scud" and suspended by his piercings from the chandelier so long as he helped generate funds for their precious cause. This, therefore, was her dare:

They would each dress in a bespoke gown by their favorite couture designer—Desdemona's by Ernanda, Chaz's by Manu Lirhu. At the auction tables, they would give bidders a chance to vote on whose ensemble was the more spectacular. The loser would donate the worth of their gown to the Factory Girls with Phossy Jaw Charity. The winner would buy the loser a drink of their choice the moment they were emancipated from their offices.

Reluctantly, Chaz had agreed. But he soon grew enthusiastic. For months now, they had been planning their gowns, meeting in secret with their designers and obsessing over minutiae, each boasting how entirely they would cast the other under their glittering shadow.

And then—after all that!—Chaz had not materialized. Not till now, anyway, when Desdemona's duties were all but done. An awful night it had been, too. She had thought she would be bored. Instead, Desdemona felt scraped raw, with a headache behind her eyes and at the back of her neck. Her mother was a loudmouth, a scab-ripper, a visionary. Tracy Mannering did not care to wrap fine lace around decay; she wanted *everyone* to see the purulence. And now Desdemona would never be able to *unsee* it.

Across the foyer, Mrs. Mannering's trumpeting tones sobered to a deeper bassoon.

"As you know, Seafall's most *intrepid* young journalist,

Salissay Dimaguiba, wrote a *fearless* exposé last year on the *insalubrious* conditions these young women daily endure in their work environment. It provoked such *outrage* among our community that I—with my dear friend and colleague Audrey Alderwood—organized the Southern Leressa Convention Respecting the Prohibition of White Phosphorous in Matches."

"What a button-popper!" Chaz's clove-sweet breath tickled Desdemona's ear. "Don't her secretaries edit her speeches?"

"No one edits Mother."

Mrs. Mannering's speech rolled on: "*All* proceeds from your generous donations shall go toward the construction of a new ward at the Seafall City Working Women's Almshouse!" She paused for more applause. "The ward will be dedicated *entirely* to the treatment of girls suffering from repeated close contact with the poisonous fumes of white phosphorus. Now, without *further* ado . . ." Spreading her powdered arms, she embraced the whole room and all the beaded chiffon, embroidered velvet, winking sequins, and fluttering fans.

". . . It is my honor to introduce to you the most *scintillating* stars of this evening! The young women of Albright Match Factory!"

One floor above the crowd, from doorways dotting the mezzanine, the Phossy Gals trooped out. As drilled

by their hostess, they processed stiffly down the bifur-
cated staircase. The line leaders stopped on the penulti-
mate step above the smooth tile of the center landing.
The others paused behind them. Suspended in motion,
hands resting on the marble banisters, these jaded and
decaying flowers peered out from their tiered garden to
meet the gazes of their benefactresses below.

Desdemona was too far away to perceive details, but
thanks to Mrs. Mannering having foisted their acquain-
tance upon her earlier in the greenroom, she could imagine them clearly. Their faces twisted by osteonecrosis.
The stench of infection rising from their abscesses.
Swollen joints, collapsed jaws, exposed bone, barren
eyes. Some wore neck and back braces to bear up their
frames, because their disintegrating skeletons could no
longer do so—very like, and also horribly unlike, the
gilded caryatids of the Seafall City Opera House, which
looked decorative but carried the weight of the painted
roof upon their naked, golden shoulders.

The Phossy Gals ranged from mid-teens to mid-
twenties, the oldest being about twenty-seven—Desdemona's own age—though years of factory work had
so hagged the "gal" that she seemed a veritable goblin
crone, fit only for boiling babies and picking her teeth
with their bones. All the young women had been
putting in ten-hour workdays at Albright Match Fac-

tory as mixers, dippers, and boxers for the better part of a decade.

After an appreciable hush, Mrs. Mannering ascended the green marble staircase. Once more she took center stage, right in the middle of the landing, and began introducing each of the young women by name. The Phossy Gals plastered on choreographed smiles that showed more hole than teeth and resumed their slow descent down the Ceremonial Staircase. When they reached the center landing, their two lines interweaved to form a single file behind their hostess, and at her signal, they followed her (some resignedly, some defiantly) to the ground floor of the Grand Foyer, where philanthropists, politicians, and journalists waited to mingle with them.

"The cost of a more comfortable death," Chaz murmured, "is dignity."

Desdemona tossed her head. "What about any of this do you find undignified? This is probably the grandest night of their lives!" Earrings chiming expensively, she confided, "Mother agonized for weeks over whether it would be more shocking to parade her product line of Phossy Gals in ordinary homespun or drape them in diamonds and accentuate their deformities with lipstick. *I* advised the latter. If you ever throw *me* a ball to honor the half of my face eaten up by a tumor, don't let homespun within a mile of me. Aunt Audrey backed me. *She*

wanted press coverage, photographers, possibly a riot."
She shrugged. "People like diamonds. They're *dignified*."

"It's a dime museum display," Chaz countered flatly.

Desdemona sniffed. "They'll overfund by the end of
the evening."

Chaz's silence grew pointed enough to conduct sym-
phonies. But because he refrained from indicating the
obvious, that he recognized every single one of the
gowns those girls were wearing, Desdemona decided not
to claw his eyes out. She had been too embarrassed to
confess any time these last months that she—at her
mother's instigation, of course—had loaned a dozen and
a half of her old gowns to be taken in, hemmed, mended,
and otherwise spruced up for the Phossy Gals Follies.
Loaned! As if she'd ever wear them again after tonight.

She was sick of looking at them. No matter where they
were in the crowd, or how often they moved, her eye was
drawn unerringly to what had belonged to her. Those familiar shimmers of silk, flappings of fringe, twinkles of
beadwork, graceful folds of velvet . . . What did they feel
like now, on *those* bodies? Especially that hag—her age
double—with her black hair done up in a voluptuous
bouffant, just as Desdemona's was.

No. She wouldn't look any more.

She flounced in an about-face to survey her friend.
Fully prepared for an eyeful of resplendency, what she

saw instead made her frown. She blinked, thinking she'd missed something.

But she had missed exactly nothing. No wig, no jewels, no shapewear. Above all, no gown. Not even some semi-retired thing she'd encountered on Chaz on a previous occasion. Certainly not The Gown, the one that he had spent a small fortune to commission from Lirhu themself.

"What is this? A, a what? A soup-and-fish suit?" She was so shocked that she *sounded* shocked, which Desdemona did not like. But . . . that *suit*! And not even Chaz's *best* soup-and-fish suit! White tie. Black jacket, white piqué waistcoat, black patent leather shoes . . . *Boring*.

Giving her best friend the once-over for a third time, Desdemona's plucked eyebrows arched like aqueducts. Where were his peacock tails? His painted silk cravat? The Monkey Face orchid in his lapel? Chaz sported *none* of the usual stained-glass ostentation, the masterstroke of adornment, that transformed him from well-dressed into a work of art.

His face canted away from Desdemona's scrutiny, Chaz watched Tracy Mannering instead. She was introducing one of the Phossy Gals to the vice chancellor of Southern Leressa and the Federation Islands. Force of personality (and a firm grip on the arms of each party) brought these polar opposites of the social spectrum resoundingly together in a handshake. There should have been drums. Chaz even pitched his voice to be drowned out by them. "I thought my Lirhu gown inappropriate for this evening."

"How so?" Desdemona demanded. "If *my* Ernanda is appropriate, *your* Lirhu must be! Look around you. Not a single gown in this room costs under ten stacks—most of them twice that!"

Chaz sighed. "If the society aunties saw me in my Lirhu, they would laugh indulgently and consider it all a very charming sort of clowning." He worked to keep his voice even. "But to me, it is *not* clowning. *This* is." He gestured to his jacket and tie, his hair arranged in its careful slick, all those flaming curls flattened, and made a sharp gesture, as if to fling it all away. He said, forlorn as a foghorn, "And so . . . I forfeit our dare, Desdemona."

He seemed to expect a scold, or a second round of the cold shoulder. But Desdemona was already sliding out from behind the auction table to wrap her arms around his wiry, tense, boringly black jacket-clad arm. Sticking her face in the hollow of his throat, she nuzzled him until he giggled and shied away. Chaz smelled divine. She could just about murder him for his nose. He always managed to obtain the newest perfume days before it officially launched.

She announced magnanimously, "All right, Chazzy

darling. I accept your forfeit. You know I love to win! So, you'll write Mother a cheque for the Matchbox—that's what we're calling the new Almshouse ward—and I'll buy you your favorite Sophia Ampoule at the Chiamberra just as soon as she signs our release papers."

Relief plain on his powdered face, Chaz said, "Already delivered the cheque. However . . ." And here his tone shifted slyly, settled into something more artificially plaintive. "However, Desi, I don't fancy cognac tonight. No Sophia Ampoule for me. I want something . . . different."

"Oh?" Desdemona braced herself. She knew that tone of voice, what it boded. "Loser's choice, of course," she said with some acerbity. "What *are* you in the mood for, pray?"

"Rum."

"Chaz! You don't even like rum!"

"*Liberty* rum, specifically," Chaz explained with beatific blandness. "Imported from Rok Moris. Crafted to commemorate two hundred years of independence from the Empire of the Open Palm. Comes in its own case. Worked leather. Embossed." His rouged smile glinted like gentry rubies. "A limited edition: only twenty crystal bottles in the whole wide world. The Chiamberra, I've heard, has one of them."

Desdemona scowled. This Liberty of his would, at a

guess, cost her approximately whatever Chaz had spent on his Lirhu gown. Which, of course, he had *planned*!

Very well. He'd won this round. But she would not go down without a spat.

Rubbing her cheek hard enough against his shoulder that it left a smear of opalescent powder on the black wool, Desdemona pushed away from him. "You'll have your *Liberty*—and choke on it! But I'll see you in your Lirhu gown before the week's out, or I'll be damned! Bring it over to Breaker House tomorrow night. We'll raid Father's champagne cellar, have ourselves a private dress-up party. Father's going away tomorrow morning on a long vacation with the Countess, so we'll have the run of the place. No one to scold us if we slide down the banisters."

They grinned at each other.

The smugness in her best friend's face reminded Desdemona that she still had a dog in the fight. So far they were at a draw: one gown, one bottle of rum. Each costing approximately ten thousand monarchs apiece. Fair enough. But Desdemona knew something Chaz did not.

Clapping a hand to her forehead, she cried with artful incredulity, "Oh! I almost forgot!" and began pulling him around to the end of the auction tables.

"Can it possibly merit mussing me? Stop dragging, Desi!"

"Stop moaning, you wet blanket! Try to act excited—you should be! You'll adore this!" Desdemona covered his face with her ringed fingers. "No, no, don't you dare look; it's a surprise!"

Chaz's lacquered lashes curled closed against her palms. He had always been biddable, more or less. Give or take a few incidents. Now that she was about to beat him to smithereens and stomp on whatever remained, Desdemona felt a fresh rush of tenderness toward him.

"Open them!"

Taking her hands away, she watched the bleakness vanish from Chaz's round blue eyes. At the sight of the final auction item, his cheeks, under their thin layer of powder, bloomed with the double roses of reverence and rapacious cupidity.

"It's Elliot Howell's latest!" Desdemona crowed—though of course Chaz could see that at a glance. "An eleventh-hour donation for tonight's auction. I didn't tell you he'd pledged a piece because I didn't want to excite your hopes. Artists, you know. *Not* to be relied upon."

Of the two of them, Chaz was the true lover of art, a connoisseur and collector. Desdemona might rather be called "a collector of artists." She enjoyed keeping company with the knacksies and the crackerjack set; she liked their conversation, their vision, their vulnerability, their superb egos. The quickest way to an artist's heart, they say, is through their work—and Desdemona could afford the price of purchase. But most of her knowledge of that world came from Chaz. No one in Seafall, high society or low, knew that her main motivation to learn about art was for the pleasure of outbidding him at auctions such as these, of ferreting out undiscovered treasures from conservatories, universities, sidewalks, and basements before he could and then tormenting him with her ownership of them. To this end, Desdemona kept abreast of all the latest trends, attended gallery openings, and had cultivated her reputation throughout Seafall as a tastemaker. Only Chaz suspected she was a fraud. But bless his pearl-buttoned lips, he never said a word.

Now he breathed, "Is Howell . . . is he . . . is it . . . part of a new series?"

Chaz was staring at the sarcophagus-sized piece of painted wood like an altar he wished to offer libations to. Desdemona lifted her slim shoulders a scant half inch. "He didn't say."

"I had no idea the Voluptuists were working in encaustics!" Chaz raved, flushing even pinker. "I've been following the revival of encaustics ever since those murals were discovered at the Mount Ashanu excavation. But I had no idea that *he*, that *Howell* . . . ! Has *anyone* in Southern Leressa done such a thing in the last five hundred years?"

"He's the first I know of," Desdemona confirmed for

him, grinning at his pleasure and amazement. "Howell says electricity makes working in encaustics easier for him than it would have been for the artists of Ashanu half a millennia ago. He seemed a bit sheepish about it, actually."

Elliot Howell was one of the founding members of the Voluptuists, a small but strident movement in the art world that emphasized brilliance of palette and brazenness of brushstroke and incorporated phantasmagorical elements married to the mundane. Voluptuist art was a direct reaction against the last generation of Illusionists, who were obsessed with turning two-dimensional canvases into something you believed you could walk through. Illusionists endorsed the divorced reality of the three worlds. The borders were broken down, their work pronounced, the passes blocked. Every mural, every fresco, reminded you, meticulously, that what you thought was a doorway was really only a blank wall after all. Voluptuists, on the other hand, frolicked in the living guts of any world they could get their hands on, interbraiding realities in an eruption of color and motion. Legends from dusty old nursery tales, like the Bull with Five Horns, the golden-spined Keythong, the Abarimon with its backward feet, or the Bog Sisters Three, walked hand in hand with newspaper girls and one-armed foundry workers. What was vital was capturing the daily bizarrerie of a life mythically perceived.

Desdemona had first stumbled upon Elliot Howell during a shopping expedition. He was painting a street scene from a little easel he'd set up on Alderwood Wharf, his back to the water, facing the Fish Market. It was still called that, though it didn't sell fish anymore; those stinking stalls of history had all been replaced by upscale shops not even a pirate queen could afford. But in Elliot's painting, instead of high society girls like Desdemona swinging in and out of the shops laden with bags and bandboxes, there pranced a mix of goblin and gentry creatures, every one of them dressed in couture fashions showing off their scales, chitin, feathers, and rainbow-paned wing membranes. The cheek of it, the *colors*, snagged her eye. She hired him on the spot to paint her formal portrait, which she unveiled at her twenty-fifth birthday gala.

Chaz said later that he only forgave her for discovering Howell first because otherwise—and this thought kept him awake nights—he might never have been discovered at all.

Not long after Desdemona's gala, Dean Alessandra Mallister, hounded by her son, appointed Elliot Howell the artist in residence at Besant College of Fine Arts. She gave him a raise, a university housing stipend, and every encouragement to produce as much art as possible.

Soon, galleries all over the islands and mainland roared for his work. "Elliot Howell"—the newspapers leapt to quote Miss Desdemona Mannering—"is one of the greatest artists of the Orchid Age." She knew she wasn't perjuring herself to say it either; Chaz had told her so.

"Horned Lords, she's beautiful." Chaz could not rip his gaze from the painting. "What did Howell say about her?"

"Not much. He was in a rush to get back to Mrs. Howell. They have a new baby or something. That wife of his!" Desdemona shuddered. "She never fails to give me the heebie-jeebies. Those eyes! Those tattoos! Anyway, he dropped it off as is and said he hoped it would help the cause. I got the impression he was happy to be rid of it. It *is* creepy—even for Howell."

The encaustic, painted in pigmented wax medium on a wooden panel, depicted a young woman, or womanlike creature, in a cage. She was too tall and thin to be comfortably human. She looked akin to the creatures lounging overhead in the night-colored panels of the coffered dome ceiling. Her skin was silvery-green, which shimmered in contrast to the dull iron bars that imprisoned her. She had far too many fingers on her hands. Her nails were curved like sickle knives, filigreed in copper. Her eyes were the color of bruised berries, and her cobra-lily lips were slightly bared, as if about to bite. Behind her lips gleamed a set of seed-pearl teeth, sharp as a shark's. Something in her face reminded Desdemona of that Phossy Gal with the black hair like hers. Some fierceness.

"She's—she's allegorical?" Chaz surmised. "Not from the gentry mythos, I don't think. See those hands? That skin? No, she'd be a goblin. Right out of Bana the Bone Kingdom. The World Beneath the World Beneath, where the desperate travel to barter for their heart's desire." He swallowed, making his white piqué bow tie bob. "I wonder why she's behind bars. You shouldn't keep goblins under iron—or gentry—it hurts them. She's hurting. Look at her eyes . . ." he trailed off.

"I know her name," caroled Desdemona, who did not care to look again at the fierceness and fury and *cunning* in those eyes. "It's on the bid sheet." She read off the painting's title with éclat. "*Susurra the Night Hag*. Sounds goblinesque to me!"

"What's the highest bid?" Chaz asked, very softly.

Desdemona told him.

She did not tell him it was *her* bid, or that what he was about to spend on the painting would more than settle the score over the rum. She also did not tell him that whatever amount of money they shunted toward the Factory Girls with Phossy Jaw Charity, it would not be enough. No more than the booze she'd shortly be consuming at the Chiamberra like a uni freshman on her first binge would be enough to assuage the guilt and self-revulsion she'd been suffering all evening. But it would be *something*.

"Triple it," said Chaz.

2

VOICES AT MIDNIGHT

JUST AFTER TWELVE, Desdemona's chauffeur dropped her off under the porte cochere. She sang out an inebriated good night and ran lightly for the door. But as she entered the vestibule of Breaker House, she froze.

Just off the front entrance to the right, the library was ablaze with electric lamplight. When she heard her father's hammer drill of a tenor, Desdemona's expression slammed closed like a portcullis. She slipped off her heels, hooked them against her hip, and glanced over her shoulder, contemplating whether to leave by the front door again. This ran the risk of drawing the unwanted attention to her exit that her entrance had not rated.

But an irritated curiosity soon melted her full-body freeze. Why was her father even here? According to his printed schedule (which Desdemona received as regularly as her mother's duty rosters), H.H. should be with the Countess in their penthouse suite at Mannering Tower, luggage packed, tickets bought, farewell till next summer. At this hour, he really ought to be lounging on the sofa in his dressing gown, toasting his mistress, and mocking the absent Mrs. Mannering, who, according to him, had only the fire of social reform to warm her bed at night. (Desdemona knew better, of course. Aunt Audrey, wife of Mrs. Mannering's older brother, was more than just her mother's "dear friend and colleague.") But instead of being safely ensconced in his tower, on the eve of departing for the mainland, her father was here, in Breaker House's library, holding forth at length to some unknown person.

"I'm closing on a purchase of White Raven Island," came his clipped bray, baleful and self-assured. "Three thousand acres. Most of it dunes. Sitting idle. No one there but a bunch of inbred bug-eaters living out of their lobster pots. Papers are speculating I bought it for industrial sand mining." H.H. chuckled. "Let me tell you, boy, *that* brought down a flurry of liberals on my head. Already lobbying the Chancellery to shut me down. Lousy dirt-muggers. *Protect our precious coasts! But not out of our own pockets, oh no!* Seven hells take 'em. It's not *sand* I'm after."

He paused, as if expecting a response.

There might even have been one that Desdemona could not hear—on the other end of a telephone line, perhaps? She pricked up her ears.

"Bitumen," her father said flatly. "Crude bitumen. Coal's on its way out. World wants oil, and I want Candletown Company to provide it. After the troubles last summer over the railway, my employees at Merula Colliery took a cue from the United Locomotive Engineers. They're organizing. My own people! The Mine Workers Labor Union, they call themselves. Saboteurs. I'm paying my weight in cash for security. The Merula's about tapped out anyway. It's all become . . . unnecessary."

Another inviting pause. Another forbidding silence.

Desdemona crept closer to the library. She peered through the crack of the barely open door. There was H.H.'s broad back, bent forward. His arms were braced against a rosewood and malachite console table. He was much closer to the doorway than to the fireplace under its marble mantel, which took up most of the eastern wall. Nevertheless, that was where all of his attention was focused.

H.H. jabbed at a map on the console table. A noise like the report of a bullet. Desdemona nudged the door open another inch. Who was her father talking to? He was nowhere near the handset.

"Here. White Raven Island. Northeast of Winterbane Archipelago. Where I want my bitumen. Call it up, like you did the coal. You can deposit the oil in the sand itself—we'll extract it that way first. But I'll want to drill by and by, so make sure there's a rich reserve of crude below that. I'll pay your tithe. I've some three hundred fifty, four hundred strong men working for me in the coal mines. They'll go down into Merula Colliery in about four hours—you know where. You take your tenth of them. I'll dispose of the rest."

You opened the doors for this?

At last, a reply! From the fireplace, no less. A stranger's voice. Desdemona simultaneously wanted to wince away from and lean into it. She listened, hard. Bent all her being to listening.

"I've read the contract!" H.H. blustered, picking up what looked like a roll of blueprints lying next to the map and shaking it open. Even from behind, Desdemona could tell it was not typical engineering bond paper, but something creamier and heavier, more like parchment or vellum, highly decorated on both sides, like a page ripped out of an ancient illuminated manuscript. Flapping it at the fireplace like a red cape at a bull, he said, "The agreement—"

Was necessary in time of war, the other voice interrupted. *Signed in fire and sealed in blood. Had my ancestors foreseen it would be used to bind me thus!*

"Well, it is," H.H. sneered. "And will continue to be. Desdemona will marry one of these days, and I'll make sure her son knows the contract inside and out! You're mine to command—I've read all about it!" he said again. "So long as I offer you fair trade, you *have* to deal with me."

The voice that was a brand that was a scar that was an ache did not reply.

H.H. snorted into the eloquent silence. He tried to roll the hunch out of his shoulders, for he was not a man who cared to cower, but his body would not unbow, and he held the contract before him like a shield. But what was in the fireplace that frightened him so?

A glimmering beneath the mantelpiece caught Desdemona's gaze. Like a head turning her way. A glint of green—eyes narrowing in close attention. She saw his shape then. Tall, and . . . thin. Ludicrously, inconceivably, *irrationally* thin. A ribbon of smoke. A strip of black silk. The glow of live coal, if one burned emeralds for fuel instead of carbon.

Are you your father's daughter or your mother's?

He was talking to Desdemona, from the fireplace in Breaker House's library. For her ears only. If "talking" could describe a voice that was almost pure seismic activity, a roaring pillar of nearly invisible fire.

H.H. was still droning on like a helicopter powered by hornets, but his words did not seem to penetrate. Desdemona stared past his hunched shoulders, into the fireplace, into the flames that were not flames. Too white.

Too black. Feeding on nothing. Illuminating nothing. Brilliant all the same. Were those his eyes? Was he waiting for an answer?

Minutes ticked by. The question hovered in the air between them.

Are you your father's daughter or your mother's?

She did not know how to answer. And then she had no more time, for her father had crumpled the map on the console table with one hand and was shaking the rolled-up contract with his other, roaring, "Bitumen! Rivers of it! Make the White Raven run black with it! Kalos Kantzaros, King of Kobolds, hear me! I, Harlan Hunt Mannering, command you. Take as many miners as you want in exchange. I don't need them anymore. They are the tithe. *That's* the bargain."

His words seemed to complete some ritual. The crushing, comfortless attention of the fireplace snapped away from Desdemona. Something happened to the flames. Something green.

Hardly breathing at all, Desdemona backed away, all the way into the vestibule. Then, dashing through the dark expanse of the entrance hall, she fled up the marble staircase. Her bare feet left damp smudges on the stone steps. They disappeared like ghosts in her wake.

3

CANDLETOWN COMPANY DISASTER! 356 SOULS LOST!

DESDEMONA SPREAD BOTH HANDS flat over that morning's copy of the *Seafall Courier*. They did not tremble. She inspected her nails, still glowing from yesterday's manicure. On her left hand, she wore two rings of amber, one her right, a ring of smoky topaz. Her left pinkie tapped the headline.

She read the article through twice: headline, byline, lede, body, conclusion, then straightened up on a sharp inhale.

It was the first breath she'd drawn in a minute and a half. The gasp hurt her lungs but cleared the black spots that danced like typeface across her vision. Moving like an automaton, Desdemona picked up the phone and rang her father's office.

His secretary answered, of course; H.H. was gone that morning to the continent with Countess Lupe Valesca. They were traveling deep inland to one of his properties, a villa on the river island of Kalestis, where it would take relay couriers or possibly signal fires to reach him.

Desdemona knew this. Just as H.H.'s secretary knew it was Desdemona when she asked, without announcing herself, "What happened?"

The secretary, an efficient young epicene named Landry, who lived for their work, never slept, sweated, fretted, or ate—or didn't seem to, at any rate—answered right away, smoothly.

"Our official position, Miss Mannering, is that we do not know. There was an explosion at Merula Colliery. Coal dust. Possibly firedamp. No one can say with certainty. All the witnesses are dead."

"When you say *all* . . ." Desdemona velveted her alto to a low burr, letting the ellipsis telegraph her fury. Chaz might have run from such a sound. But Landry, accustomed to H.H.'s fusillades of perspiring outrage, did not hear any significance in her pause.

"Three hundred fifty-six workers went into the mines at four thirty this morning."

"How many have been recovered?"

Landry's pause throbbed. "Expert rescue teams are being brought over by rail from Southern Leressa. We'll know more shortly."

Desdemona's voice sank even lower, like some golden

beast of the veld catching sight of a passing herd. "Oh?"

"Before he left, Mr. Mannering ordered his foremen to seal all the pitheads to contain the fire. No rescue efforts have yet been made. We are to wait for the professionals. Right now it's too dangerous to attempt any rescue, especially when it is unlikely there are any survivors."

"I see. In your next telegram"—Desdemona smiled all the way through the phone, as if she could somehow shove her rictus through the wires down Landry's graceful throat—"please congratulate my father on an *impressive* tithe."

"I beg your pardon, a what?"

She hung up.

~

That morning, Desdemona ate her breakfast off delicate porcelain inherited from her great-great-great-grandmother, Lataisha Mannering. Her espresso was hot, black, sweet as syrup, spiky with cardamom, but she could not taste it. Two things haunted her: her dream from last night—looking into a mirror and seeing in her reflection a festering Phossy Gal all carved up like a turnip lantern on Gentry Moon, her disintegrating mouth stuffed with burning matches—and the nightmare she'd woken to this morning.

Three hundred fifty-six workers went down this morning...

Putting her demitasse down, she submitted to her maid's deft hand with a hairbrush and stared into her own eyes in the mirror, wondering at the stranger who stared back.

"We'll do an upsweep today, Miss Mannering," said Ranli.

Her soft voice, with its hard-rolled *R*s and slim *L*s, barely made a dent in Desdemona's concentration. Ranli was Leechese, an immigrant to Seafall. She had unerring taste in all matters sartorial and tonsorial and supported three, far younger, highly decorative husbands on her not inconsiderable salary, while they kept house and raised their children in one of the gaudier, cheaper boroughs of the city. Chaz kept trying and failing to hire Ranli away. He was not the only one of Desdemona's friends to attempt this, but he was the only one who regularly almost succeeded. Ranli's wage was unspeakable. Worth every last gilt penny.

"Pompadour with a low cottage loaf," Ranli continued. "A few loose coils. The white felt hat, of course, with brown velvet trim and pom-poms. You'll be visiting today?"

Take your tenth ... I'll dispose of the rest ...

"Yes," Desdemona answered absently.

"The brown corduroy trotting suit, then," Ranli informed her with regal efficiency. Ranli never wasted words with her employer. She had been hired for her opinion in exactly one field—and in that field, her opinion was law. "With your baum marten boa and muff. It's a chill day, and lowering."

Are you your father's daughter or your mother's?

Restless and listless by turns, Desdemona replied, "Yes, the furs. Heap me up in dead things. I need all the creature comforts today."

Ranli, her spine straight as a scepter, disappeared into the dressing room to fetch the selected items while Desdemona toyed with the demitasse, staring into it as if trying to see through worlds.

"If the World Flower is real . . ." she murmured, hardly believing she was saying the words aloud.

If it was real—Three Worlds theory, gentry tales, all the stories of goblin ghoulies dwelling in the World Beneath the World Beneath—then early that morning, just after midnight, her father had *sold*, to a blaze of black-and-white light in his fireplace, thirty-six of his own Candletown Company employees in exchange for a load of bitumen on White Raven Island. *Then* he manufactured a mining incident to murder the other three hundred twenty-one to cover up the missing men.

You take your tenth of them . . . I'll dispose of the rest.

Desdemona thunked down the demitasse. The dregs of her espresso sloshed over the rim, spraying the newspaper beneath it so that it read, *CANDLETOWN COMPANY DI*—splotch—*STER!*

A tithe was a tenth, was it not? And her father, whom Desdemona had always known to be rude, ruthless, amoral, and brutal, but whom she had never imagined could murder hundreds of men with a shrug of his shoulders, had done just that. And for what? For oil?

She looked down at her hands.

For oil. For the porcelain place setting in front of her. For the lace waterfalling down the sleeves of her dressing gown. For this room, with its silk linens, its lustrous mohair velvet upholstery, its jacquard coverlet, and the vanity of lacquered ebony and shagreen. For the Aniqua Adrian perfume she wore at her inner wrists. For her amber and topaz rings. For people like Ranli to do up her hair.

Feverishly, Desdemona clawed the rings off her fingers. They rained onto the patterned silk-and-wool carpet like precipitation from a gentry sky, which lets fall jewels and coins and pearls on the virtuous, but snakes and centipedes and toads on the wicked. So the stories went.

She glanced up. Winged heads of plaster gentry babes festooned every corner of the ceiling, but not a single toad did they spit from their leering mouths. No, the toads were all in her belly, agitated and slimy. Sweating out the stuff of hallucinations.

If it was real . . .

Desdemona glanced around the room, her eyes wide, her breath coming in fast.

. . . then these walls could be *doors*.

There had always been stories about Breaker House. It was, so the stories went, one of the last thresholds between worlds. Every night at midnight, there was a far-off sound of bells (bells made from the bones of lost mortals, they said), and the walls of Breaker House opened into the next world below.

That world was the Valwode, where the gentry lived. In the Valwode there was another Breaker House, called Dark Breakers, the seat of the Gentry Sovereign.

Desdemona had not read gentry stories since she was a child. Even then she was more interested in sports and pranks than books. But thanks to Voluptuist artists like Elliot Howell, who had taken to reinvigorating World Flower mythos through their media, she was fairly familiar with the players.

Howell often used his creepy wife for a model when depicting the Gentry Sovereign. He painted the tiny, terrifying woman as a powerful queen with a crown of antlers bursting from her brow, or sitting on a throne made of a hundred crescent moons, or limned in stars as if extruding them from her skin.

After attending Howell's first-ever gallery opening in Seafall, Chaz had gone directly home and spent weeks poring over all his old nursery book texts, subjecting Desdemona—whenever she came over to drag him back into the light—to endless lectures about the Gentry Sovereign, "Queen Nyx the Nightwalker, who ruled the gentryfolk by dreaming the very Valwode into being, over and again, so that it never died." Her royal seat, Dark Breakers, apparently opened onto another world even deeper down, a midnight realm, where stood *another* house called Breakers Beyond. This house resided in Bana the Bone Kingdom, where lived Erl-Lord Kalos Kantzaros, King of the Kobolds, and all his goblin court.

Kalos Kantzaros, King of Kobolds, hear me! I, Harlan Hunt Mannering, command you.

Desdemona pushed back from her chair and stood. Then sat again, uncertainly. Her hand hovered over the handset of her telephone, like a phantom deciding if a particular object was worth haunting.

Are you your father's daughter or your mother's?

The headline stared up at her from beneath a spreading circle of espresso, bleak as her own eyes in the mirror.

35— S—ULS —OST!

Her fists clenched.

Take as many miners as you want in exchange . . . They are the tithe. That's the bargain.

It was true. All of it. Her father was a murderer, Desdemona his witness. She had let this thing happen. This massacre. She was complicit.

The *Seafall Courier* splatted against the wall—a pigeon flying full speed into a windowpane—and fluttered to the floor. Gray and white. Desdemona snatched up the phone and spun the rotary dial with cold but steady hands. A moment later, a voice on the other end of the line said, "Hello, this is the Howell residence. Nixie Howell speaking."

"Mrs. Howell? This is Desdemona Mannering. Could you—are you free for lunch?"

4

LUNCHEON AT THE CHIAMBERRA

MRS. ELLIOT HOWELL sipped freshly squeezed grapefruit juice from a crystal glass and studied Desdemona curiously over the rim.

Desdemona swallowed. Cleared her throat. Gave it the old Mannering bravado.

"So. Mrs. Howell. You're . . . you're Nyx the Nightwalker, Dreamer of the Valwode, Most Eminent and Reverend Sovereign of Dark Breakers, and Queen of the Gentry. I presume."

"Queen-in-Exile," Mrs. Howell corrected her, without missing a beat. "I am retired. A thousand years of dreaming makes one so long to be *awake*, you understand. Even if it means deciding on the day of my own death."

Was that a joke? Desdemona never could tell if Nixie Howell was joking. The woman always made her uncomfortable. She stared across the table, a vast and sparkling expanse of crystal, gold, silver, and damask, and frowned.

At first she thought sourly that Mrs. Howell looked like

no queen she had ever imagined. But the longer she looked, the more Desdemona realized how, at every prior encounter with Mrs. Howell, she had allowed her gaze to willfully sidle past her face. Never once had she looked Mrs. Howell right in the eye and seen the obvious: her uncanny nature. From her eyes—the bottomless black of ink, with no whites showing, but which, when she tilted her head, showed a startling flash of azurite—to her hair, a peculiar glow-spill of ebony-indigo, plaited into hundreds of ropy braids that swung over her shoulders and down her back, shining with the sheen of starling wings—to her face . . . Her face! Like a great-grandmother who, in her extreme eld, resumes certain aspects of a little girl again, both in mockery of and homage to her youth.

Mrs. Howell's dark brown skin was dotted all over with small inkblot tattoos that danced, as Desdemona watched, in infinitesimal patterns, like the wheeling constellations of an unknown sky. The marks were everywhere. Her face. Her throat. Her hands. Her nails were long, blue-black, curved, filigreed in silver.

Taking another deliberate sip of grapefruit juice, Mrs. Howell raised her eyebrows at Desdemona and winked.

Desdemona dropped her gaze to the figured tablecloth, studying it like a fashion magazine. The Chiamberra always set a luscious table. The linen was the royal ultramarine of a late autumn sky, with silver and gold leaves figured upon it. Silver cutlery with tines and handles of plated gold glittered next to translucent dishes thin as windowpane oysters and enameled with the Bramble-and-Briar pattern, a riotous forest that came brilliantly alive under scrutiny. The longer she studied the pattern, the more Desdemona began to see the countless gentry creatures hidden amongst the flowers and tree branches. Or was it simply that now, everywhere she looked, she saw Mrs. Howell's face?

"It is just a trick," Mrs. Howell said softly. "I foreswore most of my powers. I am as mortal as you. Mostly."

Desdemona looked up again. It was no easier the second time, but she forced herself to hold Mrs. Howell's gaze. "I had no idea."

One corner of Mrs. Howell's mouth twitched. "You had *some* idea, I think. But you are good at pretending. I am not good at pretending for fun; whatever I dream becomes real. Or at least, it did, where I once ruled. Here, I do not dream."

She removed a jeweled eggcup from the silver cruet set at the center of the table, took a small round spoon, tapped the fat end of her soft-boiled egg, and then lifted off the broken top of the shell with a knife. Her knife did not match the table set. The hilt was carved of bone or horn, dyed a wine-dark red, its steel blade mottled like rippled water. When she finished shelling her egg,

Mrs. Howell re-sheathed her knife—somewhere out of sight, below the table, and leaned over her plate to grin at Desdemona.

"It was a birthday present from Elliot," she confided. "He meant it to be a boot knife, I think. But I do not like to wear shoes. So he made me a very beautiful thigh sheath."

Desdemona could not help it; she dipped her head to stare beneath the tablecloth at Mrs. Howell's feet and gawped.

The woman was barefoot. And—what was she *wearing*? How on Athe had Mrs. Howell managed to saunter into the most exclusive restaurant of the most distinguished hotel in Seafall—past the hawk-eyed doorman, the haughty maître d', and a host of hushed servitors expert in ushering out the unwanted with minimum fuss and maximum grace—dressed in nothing but an enormous, butterfly-yellow, cast-off artist's smock, belted loosely with laundry line, her feet as naked as a peasant girl's?

However she had done it, the sight of those bare brown feet gave Desdemona something to feel superior to. Her shoes, a pair of dusty-rose pumps with silk ribbons, cost more than their present luncheon would. Which was saying something. The thought imparted courage. She cleared her throat. As pleasantly as she could, she said, "I need to get down to the Bone King-dom."

"No," said Mrs. Howell.

Desdemona looked up sharply at the word she loathed most. "Of course I do! How dare you . . ."

Mrs. Howell's black eyes flashed blue, and the angry words died in Desdemona's throat like ants under a magnifying glass.

"You need," the Queen-in-Exile corrected her gently, "to go to the Valwode. There is something there you will want—in order to travel further down."

Then she grinned again, a look so conniving that Desdemona's eyes unfocused. When she could see clearly again, she was absolutely *certain* that Mrs. Howell's constellation tattoos had rearranged themselves.

"What"—she licked her lips—"what do I want in the, the Valwode?"

"Ah. We will come to that. First, you must solve the problem of getting there." Mrs. Howell made a face of friendly doubt, accompanied by a shrug, as if to say, *Worth trying, anyway.*

Desdemona lifted her chin. "Apparently the walls of Breaker House become somewhat . . . flexible . . . at midnight. But—I've been spending summers there my whole life, and I never saw them do anything extraordinary!" She leaned in. "How do I get through?"

Mrs. Howell laughed like cellos laughing. "You are not a poet!"

"A poet?" Desdemona sat back. "Well, of course I'm not!"

She was the *patroness* of poets. Poets worshipped her, curried her favor, vied for the honor of presenting their verses at her literary salons. A dedication "to D.K.M." beneath the title of a sonnet might garner its author a publication credit in the society pages of the *Seafall Courier*. Miss Desdemona Kirtida Mannering's word could be the making or breaking of a poet's *career*. But she did not write the stuff herself. The very idea was absurd!

Desdemona breathed out through her nose, like her mother did while pouring tea for a politician she did not care for but knew could be *useful*. Toying with her fork, she rammed a raspberry through a dollop of cream and said reasonably, "Elliot isn't a poet. He's a painter. Yet *he* went through—obviously."

"Obviously," Mrs. Howell agreed. "And countless others have gone through, too—even after the boundaries were all but closed. *They* had something the gentry wanted."

Desdemona's moniker at uni had been "the Anthracite Princess," referring as much to her glittering implacability as to her position as Candletown Company's sole heiress. She had always taken pride in it, and a certain refuge. But now she felt her carapace of insouciance begin to crack. She thought of the fires raging beneath the sealed pitheads of Merula Colliery. Her face flushing with that heat, she hissed, "My business is not with the *gentry*. My *business* is with . . ."

"With Erl-Lord Kalos Kantzaros, King of Kobolds." Mrs. Howell lifted a thin slice of rye bread heaped with dilled gravlax and mustard sauce to her mouth. "He is my brother. My younger brother, give or take a century as a mortal lives and dies. Last night, your father forced him into a trade for oil fields on White Raven Island, and now you wish to take back that trade. To barter with him and win the lives of those thirty-six men for yourself. You see"—Mrs. Howell smiled invitingly—"I still keep my finger on the wild pulse of our three-petal flower. An ancient habit, I fear, that will not die till I do."

Desdemona closed her eyes. "Please," she said. "If you know so much—you must know how to help me! Please help me!"

Mrs. Howell laughed. "There! You do know your courtesies! I can see why Elliot likes you, against his instinct for self-preservation. Or, perhaps I should say, why he enjoyed *painting* you. You have so many teeth and claws, I wager you cannot turn over in your sleep but you draw blood." She added approvingly, "That will stand you in good stead where you are going."

Opening her eyes again, Desdemona pushed crystal and cutlery aside. "Please tell me *how.*"

Mrs. Howell set her hands on the table, palms flat against the embroidered linen. Her eyes were like two pinwheels: coal, cobalt, coal again. Three star clusters arched in a bow above her brow. A spiral galaxy whirled minutely on her right cheekbone.

"You will need all your wits, Desdemona Mannering, all your scimitar wiles, to bargain with Kalos Kantzaros in Breakers Beyond. And you will need an edge. Something to hold over him in negotiations. Your family has used him ill these many generations, and he will not look kindly on any boon you beg of him."

"What does he want?" Desdemona demanded. "If you know something he wants, and how I can get it . . . Do you know?"

"Oh, yes." Nyx the Nightwalker's smile went a thousand years deep. "I know what my brother wants most in all the Three Worlds. The question is," she asked, "will *you* do what *I* need, in return for this information?"

Desdemona realized she had balled her hands into fists, and forced them to relax. "Yes. Whatever it is, I'll do it. Only tell me how to get to him. And how to get those men back."

"Two years ago"—Mrs. Howell returned to her lunch with great vigor—"I imprisoned my brother's youngest daughter in my court at Dark Breakers. I did not want to do it—Susurra the Night Hag was my chosen heir—but she gave me no choice."

Desdemona blurted, "*Susurra the*—the subject of Howell's newest encaustic?"

"The very one! He met her once—barely survived. Goblin girls are not notorious for their gentleness." Mrs. Howell sighed. "My niece had the wit to rule and the mind to dream—and, being goblinborn, she'd not brook any rebellious gentry mischief without immediate reprisal. I would have passed my crown to her when came the time, but—alas! For all her felicities, she was young and foolish. She betrayed me, tried to take the Antler Crown for her own before her turn. I punished her—cast her into an oubliette of iron and sank her out of sight, where no gentry creature knows to find her."

Desdemona thought she could see where this was going. She began shaking her head in denial, but Mrs. Howell ignored the cue and continued, "Susurra's prison term is almost up. But the Veil is closed to me; I cannot pass into it again. When I married my Elliot, I left the Valwode behind, never to return. Therefore, I need *you*"—she smiled her very reasonable, not-at-all paralyzing, ancient-infant smile at Desdemona, who was still shaking her head, hoping her skull would not explode—"to go to Dark Breakers and secure Susurra's release. Do this, re-

turn the girl to her father in Breakers Beyond, and perhaps then Kalos Kantzaros will give you back the lives
your father sold."

"Perhaps?" Desdemona echoed faintly. "That's all the
assurance you can give me? *Perhaps*?"

Nyx the Nightwalker flipped her palms sky-side. Her
palms were lineless. Nebulae bloomed there.

"*Perhaps* is enough to dream on. And dreams, after all,
are the substance of the Valwode."

5

CHAMPAGNE AND FURS

A POET, SAID MRS. HOWELL, is always drunk. She is drunk on words. She is drunk on love. She is drunk on ego, on her very desire to write a poem: to be transported to a place of pure experience, and afterward, in some future tranquility, to record her ecstatic displacement, confining it to precise stanzas, measured and purified and distilled to an essence meant to be shared with others, transporting them in turn. A poet is in love with the world. She is like a virus born of love; she must travel to live, and her vehicle is poetry. Was it any wonder a poet is the preferred candidate for travel between the worlds?

Desdemona was not a poet. She could not write a poem to save her life—much less the lives of the thirty-six survivors of the Merula Colliery massacre. No matter how desperate she was.

What she had, she reckoned, were the ingredients necessary to imitate a poet. A sizable ego, for one. A cellar full of champagne, for another. And she had Chaz, whom she loved. Put ego and drunkenness and love all together, and it made a recipe for poetry. Anyway, it was all she had to go on.

Chaz joined her at Breaker House at eleven that evening for, he thought, a private party. He was dressed in his Manu Lirhu evening gown and as gorgeous as Desdemona had ever seen him. Properly gussied up, girdled, cinched, and padded, Chaz had curves that she could have killed for. His gown, naturally, was a work of art: a sequined metallic ivory caftan with train, with a matching beaded bandeau threaded through his waist-length wig of red curls.

At Desdemona's request, Chaz had brought *Susurra the Night Hag* with him. His chauffeur rolled it into the room on a hand truck, propped it against the billiards table, and left with orders to return at noon the next day. While Chaz hovered cluckingly over these proceedings as though he could not bear to be more than three feet away from the painting, Desdemona poured out three flutes of champagne. Carefully setting the first in front of Susurra, she handed the second to Chaz and upended the third in a breathless tilt down her own throat.

"A fine way to treat fizz!" Chaz scolded. "How many have you had?"

"Not nearly enough." Desdemona gestured with her empty glass. "You look ravishing, darling."

His eyes softened with gratitude. His voice lost its edge. "Thank you." Twirling in front of her, he teased: "Admit it—if I'd worn *this* last night to the Phossy Gals Follies, not a single hyena in Tracy's cackle would've voted against me."

Desdemona sniffed. "I might have *paid* them to vote for you, if I knew it meant you'd buy me a *ten-thousand-monarch* bottle of Liberty afterward." She bared her teeth at him. "How was it, by the way?"

Chaz's shrug was a continuous sweep of light from shoulders to feet as his sequins flashed in sequence. "Rum is fine. I prefer cognac in *general*, you know."

"Oh," she growled, "I know. Thou gentry babe!"

Snickering at the insult, which implied the kind of mixed parentage that could have gotten you burned at the stake in centuries of yore, Chaz poured himself and Desdemona each another glass. She, meanwhile, pushed a chair against the billiards table and clambered onto it, where she stretched out on her back. Her silk taffeta trench gown was the same salmon-gold color as her champagne. Her feet were bare—bare as a Gentry Queen's! She crossed her legs and stared at the mosaic ceiling, which reeled above her gently. The billiards room, with its walls sheathed in gray-green marble, always made Desdemona feel as if she were underwater. She raked the green baize of the table with her manicured nails, smiling to think how H.H. would skin her with acorn cupules if he found her treating his favorite piece of furniture like a picnic surface.

"Hand me the cheese plate, would you, moppet?"

Chaz obliged. Desdemona selected a wedge of triple cream, a slice of hard sheep's milk, a pat of goat cheese with honey, and a mound of deeply marbled, mineral blue—"The Feisty Wold"—her favorite. A righteous heel of sourdough and a fist-sized cluster of red grapes complemented her meal. She dug in right away, viciously tearing at the bread and devouring it, crunching into the grapes, stuffing the various cheeses down in a way that was almost criminal. After all, she had no idea when—or if—she would ever eat again. At the thought, she sighed.

"What?" Chaz asked from the floor.

"Cheese," she said.

"Cheese," he agreed, gruntling into his crumbs.

Dangling her head over the edge of the table, Desdemona smiled upside-down at her best friend, who was splayed out in all his glittering glory at the foot of the encaustic. Firelight animated the pigmented wax. From behind her painted cage, the silver-green goblin girl watched intently with bruise-purple eyes. The sharps of her teeth glistened. Was she smiling? Or was that the grimace of unfathomable hunger?

I know your father, Desdemona wanted to tell her. *I met*

him in my fireplace, and he asked me a question.

I have a question for you, too, Susurra seemed to say. *Come a little closer . . .*

"What are you looking at?" Chaz asked, his voice loud as a fire alarm.

Startled, Desdemona jabbed a finger at the painting. "Her. The Night Hag. We were having a private discussion about fathers."

"Fathers?" Chaz wrinkled his perfectly made-up brow.

"Yes. She likes hers. I don't like mine. We are trying to understand each other."

"What are you talking about? Who's her father?"

"Don't you know anything?" Desdemona asked unfairly. "She's the twelfth daughter of Erl-Lord Kalos Kantzaros, King of Kobolds and all the goblinkin. She's a prisoner, and doesn't know if she'll ever see her father again. Looks horn-mad about it, doesn't she?" Flopping onto her back, she muttered, "Don't know why. If someone told *me* that spending a few years in an oubliette was a good way never to see *my* father again, I'd take them up on it in a dovetail shuffle."

Chaz's plucked brows arched in outrage. "You're off your trolley!"

"I am?"

"You're, you're making this up!"

"Why would I?" Desdemona flipped onto her side to

watch as Chaz sat up, gesticulating wildly, spilling champagne on his clocked silk stockings.

"I spent hours last night scouring my library for any mention of Susurra the Night Hag. *Hours*. I have the biggest collection on Three Worlds mythology in the whole city—maybe even on all the islands. You know what I found on her, Desi? Doodly-squat. Now you, you can't just get me drunk and make pronouncements about the nomenclature of aesthetic symbolism like some iconographic expert on the Voluptuist movement. Cite your references!"

Desdemona kicked her legs up in the air. A crinklefall of pinkly gold taffeta rustled into her lap. "Nixie Howell."

Chaz leapt to his feet, his skirts a fuming boil of gleaming ivory. "Poppycock! You can't stand her. You leave any room she enters. Now I'm to believe she's giving you lessons in obscure Three Worlds allegory?"

Desdemona giggled to keep from crying. How beautiful he was! How darling! How much she would miss him.

"That's all in the past, Chazzy. Mrs. Howell and I are fast friends. Why, we dined together today at the Chiamberra—and you wouldn't believe it, but the maître d' *bowed her out* when she left! As if she weren't barefoot and wearing a dishrag for a dress besides!"

"I believe it," Chaz replied dreamily. "She has brio."

"I have brio!" Desdemona retorted.

"Not like her."

"Humph." With some difficulty, Desdemona extricated herself from the embrace of the billiards table. Her plate fell to the floor; she left it where it lay. "Wish me luck!" she sang out, setting off across the room at a pitched swagger.

Chaz's hand shot out to grasp her ankle. "Where are you going?"

"To the lav. Where'd you think?"

"Don't know." His voice sounded disconsolate. Far away. "I don't know, Desi."

Kicking his hand aside, Desdemona stepped lightly on his forehead with one bare foot. "Don't worry, snookums. I'll be right back."

"Will you?" he asked plaintively.

"We still have half a mag of champagne. 'Sides. S'not twelve yet."

His voice trailed after her. "What happens at twelve?"

"I turn into a poet!"

~

She did use the lav, but mostly she wanted an excuse to be alone for five minutes with the telephone in her dressing room. She contemplated the rotary dial and sighed. Everything was always just the smidgiest bitty harder after—how many now?—X number of flutes of champagne. Flushing the toilet. Brushing her teeth. Now this. But it had to be done. A poet was brave. A poet called her mother on what was potentially the last night of her life.

"Ring," Desdemona muttered as the phone rang. "Ring, ring, ring."

According to the scandal rags, Mrs. Tracy Mannering lived all alone in a two-bedroom flat, cooked her own meals, and answered her own phone. But Desdemona had never caught her mother home alone, not once, any time she randomly dropped by for a visit or rang her up on a whim. Tracy was always surrounded by relentless women and so busy with her charities and organizations that she only ever ate out, writing her meals off as a business expense. The only thing Desdemona had ever seen in her mother's zinc-lined icebox was a lone jar of olives. If it wasn't Aunt Audrey answering Tracy's phone, it was some other fashionable suffragist with a G & T and an agenda.

"Hiya! Tracy's house! Who's this?"

Just her luck. Her mother's personal assistant—the youngest hyena in the cackle.

"This is Tracy's daughter," Desdemona mumbled. "She home?"

"Probably. I think. Unless she went out—Trace? Hey, Tracy!" A second later she chirped, "One mo'.

She's comin'. Dolores, right?"

"Desdemona."

"That's right. Here she is!"

"Desdemona."

Her mother's normally welcoming bugle was a trifle wary. Desdemona rarely called, and usually only for favors or for money or to beg off from some onerous duty Tracy had inveigled her into. Desdemona leaned her forehead against the mouthpiece. She grasped the handset in both hands as if it were some slender neck she wanted to strangle and knocked the receiver against her forehead like she wanted to bludgeon herself to death.

Strident but tinny, her mother's voice called out through the line, "What's wrong? What's that sound?"

Settling the phone against her ear again, Desdemona breathed heavily into the mouthpiece. Finally, she said, "You read the papers."

"Every morning," Tracy replied, briskness replacing her concern. "The *Seafall Courier* and the *Leressa Gazette*. The world is a war zone, Desdemona. We must arm ourselves with knowledge!"

"The *worlds*," Desdemona corrected her mother. "The *worlds* are war zones. All three of them. Right? *Right*?"

"Are you . . ." Tracy paused and said forebodingly, "Desdemona, are you *drunk*?"

"Since when are you a teetotaler? No, don't answer.

Tracy," Desdemona said seriously, "tell me truthfully. Do you know about H.H.'s deal? No lies now, or I'll scream."

Tracy paused, as if collecting her thoughts. "His deal? Which one? Your father has so many—most of them as foul as his cigars."

"*The* deal, Mother. The Mannering deal. The deep one. There's a contract," she said, "an old one, with illustrations, and a voice in the fireplace, green fire, earthquakes, and something, something about calling up coal—at first it was coal—but now it's oil, H.H. wants oil on the island, and he's traded, he's *traded*—"

"The tithe." Her mother's voice was low. "Yes. I've seen the contract."

"What?" Desdemona said stupidly. "You mean you *know*?"

She had not, she realized, believed her mother could know. Or knowing about it, believe in it.

"It's one of the reasons I . . . I left him. Finally. He keeps the contract in his safe. He thought I didn't know his combination, but of course I did. I was looking for his correspondence with the Countess one day—I needed evidence, grounds for a divorce. I never found them, but I found that. Unfortunately, he caught me. And explained. At length." Her voice was grim.

"How could you . . . how could you let him . . ."

"Desdemona," her mother said more firmly, "there are

twenty women in my apartment right now, organizing staffing for the Southern Leressa Convention Respecting the Prohibition of White Phosphorous in Matches, all paid out of my pocket. Another dozen are coming tomorrow to help me make signs for our march outside Merula Colliery, protesting the gross delay of the rescue effort. I do what I can, and I use your father's provision funds to do it. As a moral counter to his reprehensible policies, it is never enough. But I had to decide—a long time ago—that my concern is for *this* world. The one I'm leaving to you and to future generations. Any other world will simply have to take care of itself."

"But . . ." Desdemona shook her head, forgetting her mother could not see her. "But they're not really separate, are they? Not when, when the miners . . ."

Somewhere behind her mother's sigh, a chorus of women shouted Tracy's name. She called back to them that she was coming.

"Desdemona, I have to go now." Tracy paused. "Try to get some sleep. I'm sure you'll feel better in the morning—when you've slept it off."

"I'm sure *you'll* feel better," Desdemona countered, "when you wake up tomorrow and I've gone to the deep."

"Well," Tracy said dryly, "if you're going to go stampeding through worlds, Daughter, the best maternal advice I can offer you is: dress warmly."

Desdemona ground her teeth. "You bet. Bye, *Trace*. Have fun on your little march. Maybe bring a few of your favorite Phossy Gals. They make good press!"

She slammed down the phone. When it started ringing a few seconds later, she ripped the cord out of the wall socket and threw the whole telephone across the room. Then she went to her wardrobe.

~

Desdemona paraded at a stately pace into the billiards room, trailing every fur she owned. There was the baum marten boa and muff she had worn on her rounds today, her favorite mink scarf, her belted coat of silver fox fur with twenty tails scalloping the hem, her sable collar and cuffs, a circular cloak of green velvet lined with chinchilla fur, a weasel wristband, an otter-skin cloak, an opera cape lined in swansdown, and a monumental beaver hat with enough sweeping ostrich plumes to fly away with. Chaz doubled over laughing at the sight of her. He was still upright, though listing alarmingly, trying to refill their champagne flutes from a bottle so large he had to hold it in both hands.

"Desi, my dearest, what *are* you wearing? You look absolutely ridiculous!"

"It's cold underground," Desdemona said with great, if muffled, dignity.

"Underground?"

"Where the miners are."

He blinked at her and said slowly, "Desi. You're frightening me."

"Look." Desdemona thrust a piece of damp and crumpled newsprint, torn from the late afternoon edition of the *Seafall Courier*, into his hand. "Do you see now? Do you understand?"

Chaz looked it over. "It's a list of . . . names. Oh."

She waited.

"Yes, I read . . . I read about this." He folded the paper very carefully and handed it back, whispering, "Those are the names of the men who went into Merula Colliery this morning. Aren't they?"

"Yes." Desdemona tucked the paper safely away in one of her many fur pockets. "I have to go find the ones who are just missing."

"Desi. Sweetheart, H.H. sealed the mines. Those miners, they're gone now, no one could have survived . . ."

"They did! They had to! Some of them!" Desdemona kept shaking her head, seeing Chaz's lips moving but refusing to hear him, until she grew sick and dizzy with the movement. "And I am going after them." Sweeping past him, she clambered onto the billiards table once more and looked down into the doleful eyes of her best friend. How she loved him! Desdemona had a cold heart, she knew—everyone said so—but if any kernel of warmth lay buried in all that ice, beneath all those layers and layers and layers of fur, it was due to him. Lumberingly, she knelt, held out her hand.

"Want to come? I'm on a mission. Rescue my men. Find your goblin girl. Trade her in. Back. Something. Name of the game's barter. Generations of Mannerings've done it. Some kind of contract with the Erl-King. Erl-Prince? Erl-something anyway. Details are fuzzy. In H.H.'s safe, gods damn him."

Chaz's mouth hung slack. "Are you playing? I can't tell. I can always tell. No. Are you *serious*?"

"Are you coming or not?" She heaved to her feet. "Make up your mind, Chaz—it's nearly midnight!"

Chaz scrambled to the chair. "I'm in." Draping his sequined train over his arm, he ascended the billiards table like a high priestess the steps of her mountain temple. "Where are we going again?"

"To the Bone Kingdom!" Desdemona announced grandly. "Or . . . was it the Valwode?" She shrugged. "One before the other. One after the next. Order matters, apparently, says Mrs. Barefoot Tattooed Queen-in-Exile. Well, we'll try it her way first." Throwing out her arms like a general running headlong into a bayonet charge, Desdemona stomped up and down the green baize field of the billiards table, shouting to the marble walls, "Well? Well? It's midnight, damn you! KNOCK KNOCK! Won't you take me for a poet? I'm sure I've got *something* the gentry want!"

"Open up!" Chaz sang out, laughing. "Open up, we've come to see the Kobold King!"

Two sounds responded, one near and one far. Bone bells ringing in a wailing wind. And water. Deep water. Like a mighty river rising over its embankments.

Desdemona grinned at Chaz. *It was working!* A chill wind blew back her black hair, bringing with it the perfume of deep ice and fresh flowers. Chaz's wig was plastered to his face, wet red ribbons trailing over white flesh.

"You're the best sister I never had!" she called above the crash of bells, the rushing roar of white-water rapids. "I'll see you beneath!"

"Desdemona!" Chaz lunged to grab her hand. Laughing, she gripped him back. Then, bulky in her furs and feathers and skins, she began twirling with him, tromping grapes and trampling cheese crumbs into the table, kicking the remaining half boule of sourdough out of her way. She danced Chaz around the ivory billiard balls, faster and faster, her bare feet kicking out from beneath the hem of her bubble skirt, and then she ran right up to the edge of the table, dragging him along, and leapt as high into the air as she could—and fell.

And fell.

And kept falling.

6

TWILIGHT OF THE GENTRY

THE FIRST THING DESDEMONA saw was a colossus enthroned upon a dais. And because she knew that if she looked around the room and saw anything else even half as strange, she might run screaming out of her own skin, she focused on it alone.

Human-shaped, more or less, but lacking genitalia. Nothing of its body left to the imagination. It was draped, barely, at shoulders and hips, in gold-shot cloth, shimmering now like wine, now like rubies. Its skin—shell? casing?—was hard, marble-white, patterned with branching capillaries of deepest lapis lazuli, like the proposed map of Seafall's new underground rapid transit system. Crowning its sculpted white curls was a towering tangle of antler horns. Tier upon tier burst from its skull like the chandelier in H.H.'s hunting lodge, a great circle of elk, whitetail, and mule deer antlers that dominated the ceiling.

It was the Antler Crown. That, at least, Desdemona

could identify from stories and Elliot Howell's paintings. It could only belong to the Gentry Sovereign. This towering white creature, then, was the ruler Mrs. Howell had chosen to replace her when she cast her first heir, Susurra the Night Hag, into prison.

Right. So there was that. One recognizable thing.

Feeling steadier, Desdemona took chary stock of her surroundings. That was when she saw the second thing. Or rather didn't see it. Because it—or he—was missing. Chaz had been just behind her. He had jumped when she did. Hadn't he? He always followed her; of course he'd jumped! Only . . . perhaps he had not this time. Perhaps he was still standing on top of the billiards table, looking down at the empty space where Desdemona had been. Or perhaps Desdemona was, in fact, lying on the billiards room floor with a broken neck.

Well, and if she was, no matter. She was here now. Or dead. Maybe both. And Chaz was . . .

Well, he was *not*. Desdemona would just have to go it alone, like she had originally planned.

A cramp stabbed her right behind her breastbone. Her rib cage squeezed like a fist, digging bony bars into her heart. Desdemona tore her gaze from the Gentry Sovereign and dared her first real glance around the Valwode, just in case Chaz was somewhere near.

So this was Dark Breakers, was it? The shadow of

Breaker House one world down. What had been the billiards room in Breaker House had become in Dark Breakers some kind of royal court or something: a vast chamber, faintly glowing, as if every surface reflected moonlight but from no moon she could see.

That was when Desdemona noticed the third thing. Really, she scolded herself, reeling internally, it should have been the *first* thing.

The room—or royal court, or whatever it was—was packed like one of Tracy's philanthropic jamborees. Desdemona had hurtled herself, it seemed, into the midst of a heated debate.

"Alban Idris!" called a voice near Desdemona's elbow. "You must abdicate!"

The immense white creature on the dais flinched. The movement sent a sort of mild shock wave through the room. Desdemona felt it in her gut, but did not know why. The eyes staring from that marble face at the angry crowd were wide and wet and black and deep. Even as imposing as it was, with the authority of its stature and the Antler Crown upon its head, the Gentry Sovereign had yet a cowering stillness that Desdemona associated with hunted things.

"You cannot rule us if you cannot dream us!" shouted another voice, somewhere behind Desdemona.

The flinch this time from the Gentry Sovereign was

not *visible*, but its entire body seemed to shrink back into its wickedly bright silver throne. If it withdrew any deeper into its seat, the Gentry Sovereign ran the risk of impaling itself on one of the protruding razor-sharp crescents that seemed to make up its throne. From across the room, which seemed acres away, Desdemona saw an owl-headed man leap up from the floor to perch on the shoulders of his neighbor and screech in a voice like a rusted grate swinging shut, "If you do not dream us, we will die!"

"You are murdering us!" another cried.

"Our world is sloughing off at the edges!"

"We are disappearing!"

"This is your doing, Alban Idris! You were sent to dream us! You *must* dream us!"

And yet, for all their fury—and in a room stuffed with hundreds of gentry, Desdemona could smell the fury like flowers burning on some desperate pyre—none of the creatures rushed the dais, or in any way attempted to attack. She slunk into her furs, trying to hide inside them the way the Gentry Sovereign tried to hide inside its throne, and wondered why the gentry held back.

A few months ago, during the hottest days of the "Summer Troubles," when the United Locomotive Engineers went on strike for better hours, better pay, and safer working conditions on the rails, Desdemona had seen demonstrations in the streets of Seafall with the same sense of angry urgency. At the time, she'd been sleeping with Salissay Dimaguiba, her mother's pet journalist. She'd pick up Salissay in H.H.'s Model Noir and take her cruising past the picket lines, the ULE headquarters, where union leaders met to organize, the police station, where officers in riot gear readied their horses and hitched up their paddy wagons, and even Titan Row, where the millionaire magnates of industry lived—anywhere Salissay wanted to go to get her scoop. Months of protests, arrests, several "accidental" deaths, even a bombing later, and at last the ULE celebrated what they called their Harvest Victory.

Desdemona had not marched among them—she would never willingly open herself up to any more of her father's contempt or her mother's enthusiastic volunteerism-by-proxy—but she had seen the rage and determination in their eyes from behind the windows of her automobile. She saw it again now, in the gentry. That female-looking thing with two horns of freshwater pearl where her eyes should have been; that tiny, two-headed child sporting a double ruff of rainbow plumage about the neck and little else; those three green sisters with identical long silver hair, each dressed in soft gray leathers and armed to the teeth with skinners, gut hooks, folding saws, and flensing knives, with thick stone machetes strapped to their backs... Everywhere she looked, Desdemona saw a people angry enough to kill. And yet, they did not move.

Civil protest? In the *Valwode*?

Surreptitiously, Desdemona peeked around for signs of mounted policemen in riot gear, armed with clubs and bats. She did not find them. What she found instead were dozens of cold, silent giants, each—like the Gentry Sovereign itself—seemingly carved of living stone, each as tall as a monolith, studding the restless crowd like land mines.

It was easier for Desdemona to think of them as policemen, rather than her initial reaction, which was to think of them as gods. They were *enormous*. Very like, in fact, the twelve gods of the ancient kingdom Liriat who were depicted in marble at the Seafall Museum of Antiquities. Some were smooth and white, others veined in grays and greens. The shortest was well over eight feet tall. With its rough-hewn face and crimson cape and flickering eyes, which watched the crowd with a fury that matched the gentry's, it exuded a far more predacious air than its prey-like, if larger, counterpart enthroned on the dais.

Whatever they were, Desdemona had not read of their kind in books, nor heard them talked of in tales, nor found their likeness in any of the Voluptuist art she had encountered. The closest she'd come to something of their ilk were the remarkable statues her cousin Gideon, who now lived retired in the country, used to build out of clay—but he had given all that up years ago and taken to whittling. Even the gentry, who seemed to Desdemona each more fantastic than the last, apparently found these statue-like giants uncanny, for they left careful pockets of space between the giants and themselves, even at the cost of crowding each other.

But none of those deliberate spaces were as large or as painfully described as that which separated the Gentry Sovereign from the rest of its court.

"This cannot continue, Alban Idris!"

This shout came from Desdemona's right. She turned to look, and sucked back a gawk. The roly-poly creature was as bald as an eggplant, and as purple. She had no legs, but split off at the waist into a nest of black eels. Round, pinpricked eyes and gaping fangs took the place of her feet. She slid about on a slick of purple guck that her eel-fare oozed beneath her.

"The Valwode shreds at its boundaries," this eely creature continued. "Nyx the Nightwalker's *true* successor would give us *new* dreams. She would *expand* our boundaries, quicken our nurseries, call down new stars, new storms, *renew* us. But we waste away. All we have are our own memories of ourselves, and these we are fast forgetting. The feast of yesterday cannot sustain us today.

Abdicate!" she shrieked, her eel-mouthed lower half sludging her across the floor. "Choose an heir who knows our ways! A ruler not made by cursed mortal hands to subjugate and destroy us! Give us back our own and go back to your own world!"

"This *is* our world," said the Gentry Sovereign, heavy as rain clouds. "It is ours *too*. We may have been made by mortal hands, but we were quickened by gentry magic. The Valwode is ours like Athe can never be. But we would share it with you."

"You would destroy it for us—and yourselves with it!"

The Gentry Sovereign shook its antler-crowned head. At the movement, Desdemona felt another shock wave ripple through the crowd, like the electric spark of wool on a winter's day, but room-wide.

"It will not come to that." Its voice was that of an avalanche troubled by melancholy: ashamed of its nature but unable to stop itself, ultimately, from burying whole villages beneath it. "But we understand your concerns. We hear you and will consider what you say. You have our word."

"Your word is noth—"

But the angry voice stopped abruptly when the Gentry Sovereign stood.

Desdemona shivered. All the voices, she realized,

had fallen silent. All noise—the little restless movement of hair tossing, of wings shirring and fluttering,
of claws clicking or hooves stamping on tile—had
ceased. She would have tried to back away, out of that
eerie silence, edge herself from the room, but she was
wedged in by frozen gentry, and they would
not—could not—move. It was as if the Gentry Sovereign, by the mere act of standing up, had cast over
them a pall, like the velvet mantel that is laid upon a
casket to signal the end of a funeral.

Desdemona stirred uneasily, sweating under her
furs. She regretted the motion a second later, when the
Gentry Sovereign's head turned, and it looked right at
her.

"No," it said. "Stay."

The command was not directed at her, Desdemona realized (once her heart slid out of her throat and back into
its proper cavity), but at several of its policemen-like siblings. They, she now saw, had begun moving toward her
through the frozen gentry the second she showed agency
of movement, drawing edged weapons from the scab-
bards and shoulder harnesses they wore. But obedient to
the Gentry Sovereign, the policemen did not close in on
her. They also did not re-sheathe their blades. The one in
the red cape looked at her like it wanted to crush her skull
in its bare hands. Nonetheless, each returned to its orig-

inal position, resumed its unmoving stance, and stillness descended once again, as if everyone in the room except Desdemona and the Gentry Sovereign had been coffined and confined in crystal.

"Come," it said softly, to Desdemona.

7

ORCHARDS OF SILVER
AND OF GOLD

"**YOU ARE VERY KIND** for receiving me so cordially on so little notice."

Desdemona was pleased to note that her voice was warm, her hand steady on the Gentry Sovereign's arm. She felt clammy beneath her furs, and the sweet pink fog of champagne was rapidly disappearing behind her eyes, but at least she pronounced all her words correctly, and in order. Her mother would be proud.

The Gentry Sovereign smiled. "My reign here is of recent appointment, but in that time I have not seen a mortal come through from Athe. I, of course, came from there, as did my siblings. We were . . . commissioned."

"Oh?" Desdemona asked politely. "By whom? I know a lot of artists. Maybe we are acquainted."

"We do not speak his name," the Gentry Sovereign said. "When he realized we were conscious beings, that it was a gentry enchantment that compelled him to make us out of clay and then also quickened us to life, he sought to destroy us. The work of his own hands." It shook its mighty head. "If ever we leave this place and return to Athe, we fear he will finish what he started. But if ever *he* comes here"—and the marble sinews beneath Desdemona's hand tensed like folded steel—"we will break him apart."

Desdemona swallowed. She cast about for some light comment. What passed for idle chat about the weather in the perpetual pleasant twilight of the Valwode? How could she gossip without knowing any of the particulars of the court at Dark Breakers? What might this colossal, crowned ruler with eyes as sad as a dying deer's consider a compliment?

But she had trained at all the best cocktail parties of the Seafall glitterati; surely that training would not fail her now!

"You certainly have a very interesting effect on your subjects," she began caressingly. "How is it that you got that crowd of impudent rowdies to quiet down? I thought for sure I'd be thrown under their heels and stomped to death. But you controlled them so beautifully."

It was the wrong thing to say.

"Alas," said the Gentry Sovereign. "Oh, alas for that control!"

They had left the throne room together by means of a hanging tapestry, sewn—or perhaps forged—of interlocking metallic leaves: oak, maple, catalpa, ash, yew, and elm. The leaves shimmered in alternating colors, pink gold to palladium to copper, yellow gold to platinum to silver to bronze. It had parted down the middle as they approached and peeled its parts up and back, the foliage furling and curling as shy as ferns. The passageway behind it had conducted them out into an orchard of trees, each made of the same precious metals as the tapestry's leaves and twinkling under an opal vault of sky, and here the Gentry Sovereign stopped at last, pale feet sinking soundlessly into the many-hued depths of the mossery's tiles. It lowered its great head to examine Desdemona, scrutinizing her so minutely that she felt peeled of all her layers of furs.

"You are . . . not a poet?" it guessed.

"I . . . *no!*" Desdemona almost wailed. "Why do people keep saying that? Why does that even matter?" Her throat was dry, dusty from the gold and silver pollen of those impossible trees.

"Poetry might have protected you, somewhat, in this place. The gentry are as vulnerable to human art as humans are to gentry magic."

"Not *all* art, surely?" Desdemona asked, startled. She went up on her tiptoes. Though she was among the tallest of her acquaintances, this movement succeeded in extending her reach only to the Gentry Sovereign's clavicle. "I've seen some very *bad* art in my day," she whispered conspiratorially. "My friend Chaz can call it outsider art all he wants—but I say an elephant with a paintbrush has more technique."

"Good? Bad?" The Gentry Sovereign shook its head. "Art is humanity's grasp for immortality. Humans seldom live a hundred years; gentry are more or less immortal—unless they destroy each other, or self-destruct. In the Valwode, art is the only thing that can teach an immortal how to die as a human dies. The gentry have always been susceptible to it. If a human fiddler plays for them, they must dance. If a human painter paints for them, they will pine before the work, helplessly transfixed until the novelty wears off—which, for those who have the leisure, might take decades. If a human makes a statue out of clay"—here the mountainous melancholy of its voice threatened another avalanche—"and gentry magic quickens it to life, that statue will rule as tyrant in the Valwode, no matter how it wishes otherwise."

"I've known tyrants," Desdemona told it, her voice clotted with some passion she did not understand. "I saw you back there, and I don't think that's what you are."

The Gentry Sovereign shook its head sadly. "You have

not been here long. Come," it invited her. "Let us venture deeper into the orchard, that our subjects may wake from their stupor. We have found," it explained, "that when we move, we bespell them almost instantly. Art in motion. For the gentry, that is a heady thing. For you, it would be as if, accustomed to drinking a single glass of wine, you were suddenly submerged headfirst in a barrel of it."

Desdemona snorted. She was accustomed to drinking a great deal more than one glass of wine. She had even, on one occasion, filled her bathtub with pink champagne and dipped herself bodily in it.

The Gentry Sovereign continued, "But if we keep still and seated, our power is just diminished enough that our subjects may air their grievances, which are many and hard. For what the gentry say is true: we cannot dream them strong again. We cannot dream at all—we never learned!" it exclaimed bitterly. "And therefore our rule is but a rapid rush to Valwode's end. The end of the gentry. And the end of us."

The expression on the Gentry Sovereign's sculpted face reminded Desdemona of the Phossy Gals from Albright Match Factory. She saw them again with dizzying clarity, just as they had been when her mother brought her to meet them, so that they could thank her for the loan of her dresses. Fifteen girls, standing in the green-room of the Seafall City Opera House in borrowed satin and diamonds, staring at her.

Twisted faces and tumorous abscesses aside, that dying, hopeless look was the same.

Ashamed, she whispered, "I'm . . . I'm sorry."

"It seems that since our birth we have brought nothing but sorrow. But let us walk on, while there are still paths to walk."

Covering her hand with its, the Gentry Sovereign proceeded with Desdemona into the orchard. For many minutes there was no noise but the wind-chime rustle of metal leaves, the sound of their footsteps swallowed by moss. Even accustomed as she was to artifice, Desdemona could tell the luminous calm of this ever-evening air lacked vitality. There was no birdsong, no busy buzz of insects; there was not even an invisible sense of slow sap moving, fungi sporing in the sweet decay of deadfall, taciturn earthworms cycling through their brief, necessary lives just out of sight beneath the loam.

"What happens to . . . un-poets?" she asked presently, jittery in the twinkling air. "What will being in the Valwode do to someone like me? Eventually?" Would that fine drifting glitter coat her lungs until they hardened into silver and gold and she suffocated like a miner slowly dying from silicosis after too many decades underground?

"Eventually?" The Gentry Sovereign's wide black eyes

turned toward her, already wet with tears. "It will happen sooner than that. It is happening now, and you do not even realize it. Before we leave this orchard, you will surrender all capacity for thought to the drowning pleasures of your senses. Drugged by the dream of this place, you will forget your home world, your desire to return, your family, friends, beloveds, all the while sickening for the sunlight of Athe that never shines beyond the Veil. Most humans come here to do precisely that. Forget."

"I won't forget!" Desdemona protested, but her tongue tasted metallic, as if she had been licking lies. "I can't!"

"Perhaps you ought to tell us why you are here," said the Gentry Sovereign, with a soft and frightening compassion. "Just in case."

Drawing deeply of that dusty hush, Desdemona opened her mouth to tell her story but started coughing instead. The spell lasted long enough that her eyes and nose were streaming by the time she lifted her pounding head. Wiping her lips on her weasel wristband, she saw that her saliva left streaks of gold and silver on the brown fur. The shimmering dizzied her. She felt it was a secret alphabet she was on the brink of learning. "No," she said, and rubbed the wet spot out. "No!"

Glancing fearfully up into the Gentry Sovereign's patient face, Desdemona confessed everything. From her mother's Factory Girls with Phossy Jaw Charity Fundraiser, and tricking Chaz into buying Elliot Howell's encaustic at the silent auction and drinking too much rum that night only to return to Breaker House, where she overheard a conversation between her father and his fireplace, and the newspaper article about the mining disaster the following morning, and meeting Mrs. Howell for lunch at the Chiamberra, and learning that she must become a poet by midnight that night, so that she could pass through the walls and thence through worlds.

"I didn't think I'd come this far!" Desdemona burst out. "I can't afford to drown in dreams now. I have to find Susurra the Night Hag! Mrs. Howell says she's the only thing the Kobold King wants. The only thing he'll trade for. If I want to get my miners back . . ."

At her mention of Susurra the Night Hag, the Gentry Sovereign stirred restlessly. As Desdemona talked on, it began to pace, striding the wide aisles of the orchard, the rake of its antlers tearing clumps of copper and silver leaves from the trees and sending fist-sized spheres of faceted fruit tumbling from branches of galvanized gold. Only when she ran out of words did the Gentry Sovereign pause in its paces, nodding to itself, slowly, slowly, like a branch bowed under too great a weight of snow, and whisper, "If she can but be found!"

"Will you help me, then?" Desdemona asked, practically panting with eagerness, hearing the wheeze in her lungs. "Help me look for her—before it's too late? Before I forget?"

"Help you? Do you not understand?" the Gentry Sovereign cried, rounding on her so swiftly she uttered a surprised yelp. "We have searched for her already! The Kobold King sent us his ambassador when we first took on the Antler Crown, begging us to return his daughter. We gave the ambassador our full cooperation. Between us, we have torn Dark Breakers apart looking for her—to no avail. But you!"

Galloping forward, the Gentry Sovereign seized Desdemona by the fur on her shoulders, lifting her in the air like a child. "You! Nyx the Nightwalker sent *you*! At last! The Queen-in-Exile speaks from beyond the Veil! She has forgiven the gentry for backing Susurra's mutinous attempt at deposition. When she gave us her Antler Crown, she must have known the wrack and ruin we would cause. That was her vengeance. But now, *now* she declares her mercy!"

For the first time, the Gentry Sovereign smiled, wild hope illuminating its face like saint-fire. "She means *you* to find the true heir," it told Desdemona. "The Dreamer! The one who will save us. Nyx does not mean the Valwode to die after all!"

"I—I don't think you understand," Desdemona stammered. "I don't know where she . . ."

"You will. You were chosen for the task. But we must find you some protection. You are not a poet," the Gentry Sovereign reminded her worriedly, "and as you are, you will not last long. We are powerless to help you, but . . ." Again that smile. "But we know someone who can."

Desdemona's heart pounded harder in her chest. Or was it just laboring to remember how to beat?

Throwing back its mighty horned head, the Gentry Sovereign bellowed, "FARKLEWHIT!"

The response was immediate. From the air at Desdemona's left elbow there came a loud popping noise. This was followed by a fizz, a flare, a sizzling dazzle of color so bright in the mother-of-pearl twilight that Desdemona had to squint her eyes against it. And out of this fireworks display stepped a cloven-hoofed creature in a pink lace apron.

With ample belly, round biceps, round calves, and round haunches, he looked as if all his disparate parts had been sewn of very hairy, very taut, pincushions. Even his curly horns wound round and around themselves, looping tightly behind his ears and curving up again to frame a cherubic face. His horns were rooted just above the corkscrewing thatch of his eyebrows, which were in no way discernable from the rest of his hairline. Between these horns was perched a baggy, sagging, many-colored, quilted nightcap that terminated at the tip with a pompom of pulsating light, like a parade sparkler that never fizzled out. He was grinning from ear to ear.

"You called, sire?"

8

THE MIRRADARRA DOORWAY

THE UMBER FARKLEWHIT, OFFICIAL goblin emissary for Erl-Lord Kalos Kantzaros in the Valwode, beamed at Desdemona from beneath his lurid cap as the Gentry Sovereign made introductions.

"Thank you, sire, thank you—very flattering, sire," he said, and curtsied to the Gentry Sovereign. Thin black lips in a whitish muzzle formed curlicues when he smiled, the bridge of his V-shaped nose wrinkling, the corners of his eyes crinkling. His eyes were wide, mellow amber in color, split sideways with pupils like flattened black boxes. The ruffled hem of his pink apron flounced up occasionally to reveal such of his genitalia as was not obscured by the astonishing quantity of woolly brown hair that covered his body from neck to ankles. At that point, his shaggy legs gave way to a pair of hooves, obsidian-glass-black and polished to a shine that reminded Desdemona of a favorite pair of patent leather T-bars she had worn to holes at age five.

The hooves gave a clicking little caper. She laughed, and her lungs felt more her own, her vision clearing of the copper and silver flecks that floated before it. She looked directly down into the amber eyes smiling up at her and made a curtsy of her own.

"Oh, succulent and sweetly moistened mortal maid!" cried the Umber Farklewhit, with another rammy grin and a flirt of his immodest apron. "Do you, by chance, like to polka?"

"I do, in fact!" Desdemona said. Her voice came out strong and clear, unladen of ore, and Farklewhit, with that grin that split his face into hemispheres, seized her hands and swung her about, as if to dance a polka down the orchard aisles that very moment. But the Gentry Sovereign intervened.

"Farklewhit, halt. This maid has come—has been sent by Nyx herself!—to rescue Susurra! But the Valwode eats at her; we fear she has no time. We thought perhaps . . ." it trailed off, suddenly unsure.

"You want me to take her to the Mirradarra Doorway, eh?" Farklewhit bounced from Desdemona's side right up to the Gentry Sovereign. "Well, well, why not? What wouldn't I do, after all, for so ripe and knightly a maid, who has volunteered for such a perilous journey to rescue our princess—asking no reward for herself!"

"Actually . . ." Desdemona began, but the effect of the

orchard redoubled when Farklewhit moved away from her, and now her tongue felt thick and slow. Almost immediately, he was at her side again, with a cozy little head-butt to the ribs. It was quite the clout, but it knocked her brain clear again.

"All this glitter getting to you, Tattercoats?" Farklewhit asked, with a sympathetic but mischievous wink. "Good thing you're wearing furs, eh? You'd have seven hells of a time washing this stuff off your skin."

Desdemona shifted under the heavy mass of capes and coats and cuffs. She was hot, sweaty, vaguely nauseated, but she had no desire to remove even one layer. She said, muzzily, "First time I've taken Mother's advice since I started wearing lipstick. She said the world is a war zone and beauty can be weaponized, so treat all makeup like war paint."

He stroked her sable collar. "Furs are a fine look for you. Like the Wild Hunt had a hangover when they dressed you."

One of the Gentry Sovereign's cool, bloodless hands fell upon Farklewhit's burly shoulder, the other on Desdemona's. She thought the exquisite gentleness of its touch must be a matter of practice: a moment's inattention, and it could snap her collarbone like a straw. If this were a real danger, Farklewhit did not seem to fear it; his eyes rolled lasciviously and his eyelashes fluttered maniacally, and his hairy hips vibrated so rambunctiously that Desdemona began to intuit a tail somewhere beneath the apron's ribbons. She only just stopped herself from peeking to verify its presence.

"Will you help her?" the Gentry Sovereign asked Farklewhit, drawing the three of them together so tightly their heads touched. "She is our only hope, and she hasn't much time. Look into her eyes."

Farklewhit obeyed. "Duplicitous and far from innocent," he pronounced, like a doctor with a diagnosis or a judge with verdict. "I like her! We'll see what the Mirradarra can do in the way of, what do mortals call it, *protective coloration*? No guarantees, of course." He peered hopefully at Desdemona. "It might just swallow you up. But if it doesn't, you'll have free range of the Valwode, my chicken—and Bana besides—without the usual perils. Of course, it'll change you. But you won't mind that, will you? You'll hardly notice it. Mostly cosmetic."

Desdemona had no idea what he was talking about, but the power of his proximity had begun to fail her, and her knees were going soft again, running down the backs of her legs like molten metal. She was melting right down to the ground . . .

"Oops! Upsy-daisy, Tattercoats!" Farklewhit cried and heaved her over his shoulder. "That's it. Mind your cranium."

He was quite strong, his arms like knots of wood about her. Desdemona, bent in half, head hanging upside down near his rank and woolly backside—Farklewhit did have a tail, after all!—finally felt solid again.

"Go! Go!" cried the Gentry Sovereign. "Speed you on your way and back again—for if the Valwode fails, Susurra fails with it—and so do we all!"

~

There was a wood of black thorn, twined all about in vines like milk-white pythons, and a tunnel burrowing through it from one end to the other without stutter or curve. "Woodwyrm hatchling," Farklewhit informed Desdemona, during one of her brief reentries into consciousness. "You can tell by the frass. Ravenous at birth. Worse when it grows up." Other than that, Desdemona remembered little about the journey.

Later, much later, what she recalled most was the singing.

It was the flowers she was hearing, of course, their swelling silver throb, but she did not realize it at the time, jouncing like a sack of wet socks against Farklewhit's backside. The light from their petals was the only illumination in that deep couloir of thorn and vine: an eerie, low-sunk luster that shivered and chimed whenever it was noticed. Desdemona, fading in and out of consciousness, noticed. How could she ignore them? The flowers formed the endless incandescent archway through which they moved, and they bobbed and nodded, glistered and glowed at her, as if wrought from jewels by a gentry lapidary's immortal hands.

"Sopranos," Desdemona muttered.

"Like their singing, do you, Tattercoats?" Farklewhit asked her. "That's gentry magic for you! Pah! Even their *flora* is all nectar bribes and snap traps. Now, where *I* come from, we tend to go a more fungal route, and since we've hardy stomachs, we'll happily finish off a nice death cap risotto with a deadly dapperling soufflé and consider ourselves well-fed! But those flowers! Try not to listen to them too closely, Tattercoats—not till the Mirradarra Doorway gets through with you. After that, you'll be able to hum along!"

Desdemona burrowed her face into the straggly bow of his apron strings. "Never trust sopranos."

"I never do," Farklewhit agreed cheerily. "Especially ones that exude sticky mucilage!"

She dreamed, then, of all the opera singers she had ever bedded—the number was not moderate—parading past her, wearing nothing but parasitic flowers. The baritone-basses, affable and cuddly (but terribly convincing as villains from a distance); the earthy, bluestocking contraltos (the lower their tessitura, the better they kissed, though they always wanted to hold hands and discuss literature afterward); the tenors, who were not *invariably* treacherous (and were even better when they came in threes, but good luck getting them to talk about anything except themselves); and the perilous sopranos. Desdemona liked sopranos best when they were corralled en masse in her sunken bathtub, ethereal voices rising from the steam like flights of naughty angels.

"If only I hadn't cleaned my ears the other night," Farklewhit complained, bounding along, "I might've lent you the wax to stop your own! Oh well. I'll just blather on a bit, see if the down-world bray of my lusty lungs interferes with their harmonics—at least long enough to get you to the door. Where shall we start? Introductions? I feel so close to you already, what with your nose in my crack. You can call me Nanny, now we've been so intimate. Nanny Farklewhit, at your service, nursemaid to Kalos Kantzaros's twelve fiendish daughters before ever I was his ambassador. Oh, my girls! My noxious little beauties. A nest of vipers! How I loved their wickedness. You remind me of them—Susurra especially. You never told me your name, but never mind—best not say such things aloud in the Valwode. Tattercoats will do. And it suits you. You can always tell a Tattercoats by her fashion sense. That is, she doesn't have any. Now, a Tattercoats is a species of the Nine-Tails genus, from the Thousandfurs family. But if you weren't a Tattercoats, you might just be a Night Hag, like my girl Susurra. Something of the scorpion when you smile . . ."

Desdemona faded out again, this time dreaming that the crumpled wad of newsprint in her pocket, soggy and balled up like an egg, hatched three hundred fifty-six scorpions, each one bearing the name of a dead or missing miner. They crawled out of her pocket and into her furs, finding the skin beneath and stabbing her three hundred fifty-six times, then three hundred fifty-six times again, and again, and again, until she screamed and screamed for them to stop, but nothing stopped the stabbing, or the venom coursing like fire ants through her veins.

"That's right, Tattercoats. Screaming means you're still here. Screaming means you're fighting."

For the first time since she met him, Farklewhit sounded grim. Desdemona tried to open her eyes, to see what had worried him so, but they seemed to have swelled shut. She was falling apart, rotting through and through, like her mother's Phossy Gals . . .

She moaned softly.

"Keep fighting it. That's what hurts so much. If you gave in, it'd be bliss. It's hurting you *because* you're fighting it. But we're almost to the Mirradarra Doorway now. Come on. Flash some fang. Show some claw. Do like the goblins do. Never mind the gentry dream."

She woke again when her head abruptly stopped bobbing up and down in time to Farklewhit's fast trot. He slithered her off his shoulder and stood her on her feet, the rough callouses of his finger pads digging into her eyelids, cracking the hard honey-crust of pollen and precious metal that sealed them shut, scraping them free. Desdemona opened her bleary eyes to see Farklewhit's long, flat, leaf-shaped ears twitching in the gloom. He saw her staring and gave her a little push and spin.

"No time to waste. Turn around. March. Have to approach the Mirradarra Doorway on your own two feet. Them's the rules."

Wearily, she marched, the bubble hem of her pink taffeta train rustling after her, dragging up bits of moss and fern and fallen petal like a trawl. The moss gave way to paving stones under her feet: glass-smooth, sea-gray, lighting up at each footfall, and then going dark again. Black thorns caught at her hair. White vines whipped her face. The flowers sang and sang and sang.

"Is it getting darker?" she asked, her voice as scratched as her face.

Farklewhit was lost in the murk behind her. Only his heavy breathing and the heat at her back reassured her.

He said quietly, "We approach the boundary between twilight and night."

A light leapt a little distance in front of her, a green and creeping foxfire phosphorescence leaking from a cairn that was built of the same glass-pale stones as the path. The cairn, piled higher than Desdemona's head, was split down the middle by a jagged crack, like a face that was mostly mouth. Desdemona gathered her furs tightly about her, loathe to strip a single sable cuff or weasel wristband from her arms, to give up even one of her capes or collars, to unwind the baum marten boa, to shed the fox fur coat or swansdown cape or her hat with its ostrich plumes. Her taffeta gown stuck to her ribs and breasts and back. Her matted hair clung to her neck. But she was standing on her own two feet, and her mind, for the moment, was her own.

"The Mirradarra Doorway," Farklewhit announced, grandly and unnecessarily, coming up beside her. "Here, Tattercoats, you and I must part ways awhile."

"What?" She whipped around to face him. "Nanny, why?"

Desdemona felt like they had been walking together in that thorn thicket for years, that Farklewhit had saved her and therefore belonged to her, like a faithful steed or steadfast hound, and now here he was, as if they were nothing to each other, standing there and announcing he was about to abandon her—when she could barely walk, barely think, and was in no way fit to survive the treacherous heart of this unknown world!

Farklewhit set hairy hands on hairy hips. "We all have to drown alone—"

"*Drown*?"

"—but I'll find you again in the Bone Kingdom, have no fear."

Desdemona tottered toward him, fists ready, but he danced away from her. "Now, now, Tattercoats," he admonished. "I know you're braw and bellicose and your dander's up, but I've no time to play right now. I've got all kinds of arrangements to make, now we're so close. Do you have any idea how long I've been looking for my girl? I mustn't lose momentum!"

When Desdemona shouted in protest, Farklewhit raised his voice over hers, dragging the quilted cap off his head and flapping it until its sizzling pom-pom splashed sparks into her face and she stumbled back.

"Yes, yes!" he exclaimed. "I know you want me with you, but you'll likely be a while, won't you? First time going under is always discombobulating."

When she finally nodded in surrender, rubbing her sore eyes, Farklewhit shook his hat out again as if dousing a fire. The angry sizzling died down. He took a long, elaborate moment to turn it inside out. "After all, Tattercoats," he said in more conciliatory tones, "you're doing quite well for a mortal. And this being your first time world-slipping, too! Very good! Much better than the other one! All *she* does is wail and weep and call out the name *Desdemona*!"

Desdemona's head snapped up. "What?"

"*Desdemona*," Farklewhit continued with a scoff, and her breath quickened with dread and longing. "What kind of a name is that? So doleful, so dolorous, so wan and woebegone; I wouldn't wish that name on my worst enemy. But *she* seems fond of it. Keeps shouting it, any-way—and you can be sure all the demons in the seven hells are listening. Ah well. Maybe it's the only word she knows."

"Nanny—"

When his hat was all the way everted, the pom-pom popped out of the far end again and flared like a comet. Farklewhit fluffed it with his fingers, humming tunelessly to himself.

"No one understands how she got down there," he said. "She wasn't traded. Just fell through. I don't remember the last time that happened. Mostly the others don't fall quite so deep down. Now, I really must be going, Tat-tercoats."

"No, Nanny—wait!" Desdemona gathered her shred-ded thoughts about her like her furs. "This . . . girl . . . Did you see her? Was she . . . did she have red hair?"

But Farklewhit just grinned. "Come and see for yourself, Tattercoats! She's beneath with the best of us, all the way down. So jump on in—and don't get your tails in a twist!"

He turned and sprinted toward the crack in the stoneglass cairn, jamming his inside-out hat on his head as he went. Just before he passed into the cairn, he vanished. Winked out of sight, like his hat had swallowed him. But his footsteps continued on, into the darkness of the cairn. A few seconds later, there was a mighty splash.

And Desdemona knew herself to be horribly alone.

~

Inside the cairn was a grotto, and through the grotto ran an underground river. The waters were as many colors as Farklewhit's hat: blue and green and yellow and red, like a cauldron boiling over with poison dart frogs. The glassy gray ceiling hung low over the river, pitted and streaked and dripping down into enormous icicle-like crystals that quivered with an inward light. There was no path through the grotto—just a few paving stones acting as embankment to that motley river, which unspooled into the secret darkness. The waters smelled like the rot wafting from the faces of the Phossy Gals. It cackled and chortled as it slurped along the slippery banks.

She just fell through . . .

Could it be Chaz? The thought of her best friend the way she had last seen him—donkey-bray drunk and dolled up in his best dress—drove Desdemona on, though she felt her limbs failing, saw the glittering fumes rising up all around her, heard the shrill sweetness of the singing flowers. But Farklewhit's last words, like the luminous lure of an anglerfish at crush depth, spurred her upright and onward, right to the edge of the embankment.

See for yourself, Tattercoats!

Her bare feet crunched on cave-fill that crackled like tiny bones. Her teeth dug into her tongue. The taste of red iron filled her mouth. Desdemona swallowed blood, along with any puerile whimper that threatened to escape, and then she jumped into the river.

It felt like acid, going in.

And then it felt like nothing at all, as her lungs filled, and even her screams were burned away.

9

THOUSANDFURS

OPENING HER EYES WAS not as . . . simple . . . as it usually was. For one thing, Desdemona seemed to have an extra pair of eyelids. Her usual eyelids opened, and she could see through them a little, filmily—enough to know that she was no longer underwater. Then her second pair of eyelids swiped sideways, and her vision cleared.

She had a second pair of eyelids. And she could see in the dark.

She whimpered.

Some part of Desdemona's brain warned her that it was not a good idea to whimper. There were things in this world—the World Beneath the World Beneath—that listened for whimpering. Homed in on it. Pounced. Best not to whimper. Better stay quiet, stay watchful, stay alive.

At least Desdemona felt like *herself*, despite the extra eyelids and the ability to see in the dark. Much more like herself than she had anytime in the Valwode—or even for the last few days in Athe. She was sober at last—no shock or champagne or drugging dream clouding her thoughts—awake, aware, almost electric with energy.

A complete and pitchy blackness surrounded her on all sides. She knew that with her *brain*. But her *eyes* perceived the utter blackness as fine gradations of silver, precisely detailed but uncannily leached of color, like the motion picture matinees she would sometimes catch with Chaz on weekends at the Seafall Square Nickelodeon. And now that she knew she hadn't been burned alive drowning in that acid river, she looked down at herself.

And saw, very clearly, that she was naked as an ape in a nest.

Yelping, Desdemona scrambled to all fours and then scuttled up a wall. At about five feet up, she realized that she was crouching perpendicular to the floor, clutching nearly invisible handholds with fingers and feet that were padded and clawed, and that she seemed also to be in command of a multitude of tails, many of which ended in tiny, clinging claws that obeyed her will as well as her hands and feet did. At this point, Desdemona let go of everything, with everything that could possibly let go, and dropped to the floor again. Hard. None of her hands, feet, or tails stopped her. And at *that* point, she started screaming.

Hush.

Before she understood that she knew that voice, perhaps had always known it, knew it the way she knew her own heartbeat, Desdemona hushed. The black cavern flooded with light. First, a curtain of mercury came crashing down from nowhere just a few feet from where she curled in a tight nautilus of limbs, all her new tails wrapping her. Then, from the mercury pooling on the ground, there rose a flare of white flame, and out of all this leaping light and molten quicksilver, *he* stepped, the dense, starry center of the cavern's immense emptiness. The vast darkness curled around him like the arms of a spiral galaxy.

Desdemona smothered another whimper with the furred and/or feathered crook of her arm.

In the Breaker House library, he had been white fire and black flame. A glint of green. A voice, mostly. The sense of being *seen*. Now he was a tall, resplendent figure, embers sparking from his raiment like emeralds, his clothes some rich and ragged construct of unlikely elements: night-piled velvet, raven's wing, oil-spill, ebony, jet, shadow, cinder, smoke. His fingers, too long and many-jointed, were tipped with talons like smoldering gems, and upon his brow danced a crown of thallium flame.

Here, then, was Erl-Lord Kalos Kantzaros, King of

Kobolds and the Goblinkin, Ruler of Bana the Bone Kingdom, the World Beneath the World Beneath, in his truest form. His eyes—the bright shine of copper arsenite, like the satin of her mother's wedding dress—gazed down at Desdemona from a face that flickered and changed, melted, re-formed, growing new eyes, new ears, many mouths. Now he had a nose, now a beak, now a snout, now a muzzle. His long arms reached for her. His curving fingernails flickered like tourmalines. Desdemona shook her head, scuttling backward, wonder-smote and fearful, but he simply hauled her to her feet.

As soon as she was upright, Desdemona shook herself out, pushed away from him, and shouted, "You nudie-peeping lech! What did you do with my gown? It was an *Ernanda*! You think I'll find another down here?"

You forget yourself.

"And you," she snapped, "forgot to give me a towel when your river ate my dress!"

You choose your shape, not I. It is all the clothing you will ever need, here in the World Beneath the World Beneath.

Desdemona crossed her arms, and several of her tails, across her chest. "I didn't choose this! I have eyelids on top of my eyelids! I climbed a sheer rock wall—and I don't even know how! I can see in the dark!"

Desdemona Tattercoats!

When the Kobold King named her, she felt her eyesight grow keener. She narrowed her eyes but said sulkily, "What?"

But he just called out her name again: *Desdemona Nine-Tails!*

Her ears pricked up—which was when she discovered she had more than two: her own ears, and just behind them, a second pair, longer, larger, thinner, lightly furred, which perked up and flicked back. She reached a hand to touch them. The feeling was sensitive and sweet. She shivered.

Desdemona Thousandfurs!

At this her legs gave way, and her knees crashed down of their own volition, and Desdemona abased herself before him. But before she could totally face-plant, five of her nine tails slapped down to steady her. The other four started . . . wagging. Hopefully. As if waiting for a kind word or a scrap of food to drop from the terrible vision before her. As if awaiting *orders*.

Desdemona Whatever, née Mannering, Desdemona of the Nictitating Eyelids, took orders from no one, man or goblin. She flung back her head, shouting, "I have come to bargain for the lives of those thirty-six miners you stole!"

Kantzaros's laughter was as deep as any canyon that water yet wore deeper.

I paid for them.

"You *traded* my father for them," Desdemona corrected him. "And he mur—" She gagged. "—he *murdered* th-three hundred twenty, twenty-one of them. To cover his, his *tithe* to you." Turning her head to one side, she spat. "They have to go back home. They're the only ones who survived."

His head, or all the *possibilities* of his head, tilted.

Are they your friends? Do you know their names? Did you ever give them a thought before they went to their fate? Had you not overheard what you heard that night, and learned of the disaster the next morning, would you still care?

"I know their names!" Desdemona's hand moved automatically to her pocket, to that precious piece of newsprint. But she was naked. She had no pockets. The newsprint was gone, taken by the river.

"No," she whispered. She patted her new body all over—thighs smooth as mink, swansdown throat, breasts covered with baum marten fur, cream and brown and yellow, otter-sleek face, ostrich feathers streaming from her long black hair, bundle of silver fox tails springing from the bottom of her spine. "Where is it?" she cried. "Where is it?"

This?

Kantzaros opened his palm. In it, the wet, unreadable paper ball torn a lifetime ago from the pages of the *Seafall Courier*. As she watched, the ball flared up with the same eldritch witch-light that crowned the Kobold King's brow, that lit his eyes.

Desdemona leapt for it. "That's mine!"

But Kantzaros merely held the flaming newsprint aloft, out of reach, and the paper, instead of burning to ash, uncrumpled and dried. The writing on it became vivid and black again, magnified. Words began to fall off the page, hundreds of words. Names. Three hundred twenty-one of them, dripping to the cavern floor like black raindrops until only a short list remained.

Ys Dedicors
Uzami Masri
Senel Alea
Marus Caracul

Thirty-six names, those stolen survivors, danced across the page, burning a brighter and brighter green until Desdemona was dazzled by them, until they were imprinted on the backs of all her eyelids. She bowed her head and shielded her face, tears soaking through her furs.

"Please," she whispered. "Please, let me bargain for them. Please."

The Kobold King's many-jointed fingers closed around the newsprint, snuffing out the glowing names. The horns and spikes of his knucklebones shone through the liquid luster of his skin.

What do you offer?

Desdemona stopped breathing. What *could* she offer? Everything was backward! Nyx told her to find the Night Hag *first*, then use her as a bargaining chip. But the Valwode nearly killed her before she could even start looking! And now she was here, with nothing. Worse—she owed the Kobold King for her new body. Not that she'd asked for it, or wanted it. But she'd have died without it one world up, eaten by gentry flowers . . .

"I offer your daughter, Susurra the Night Hag."

He turned and stared. His features shifted beneath the thallium flame, a look of longing melting like wax into the semblance of his daughter's face, silver-green and bruise-purple, gone in a moment.

And why, asked the Kobold King in as dark a voice as he was bright, *do you think you can find her, when in all these months uncounted my own ambassador could not?*

"Because," Desdemona answered, swallowing, "your sister sent me."

The beacon of his body blazed up to a nearly lethal brightness. *You conspire with my daughter's jailer?*

"N-no," she stammered, squinting against the blaze and scrambling backward as he advanced, "I, I only asked for her help. She told me to find Susurra, and if I did, then you would, you might . . ."

But he kept crashing toward her, and Desdemona could no more stop him than she could stave off a hundred horses at full charge. But she remembered her father, bent double over the console in the library, brandishing an ancient contract in one hand and shrieking at the fireplace. *He* had not shrunk and scraped. He had insisted, repeatedly, on his rights to barter men for bitumen. And the words he'd used were . . .

Holding her hands out before her, Desdemona bellowed, "Kalos Kantzaros, King of Kobolds, hear me! I, Desdemona Mannering . . ."

But her voice caught in her throat. She could not—could not—*command* this creature. Not when she stood in his house, in the skin he gave her.

"I . . . beseech you," she said in a quieter voice. "Take your daughter as my tithe. I will find her and free her and trade her life for the lives of my thirty-six men. Accept this bargain!" She swallowed hard, for the next word did not come naturally, and added, "Please."

A pause.

An indrawn breath.

Very well. His voice was so low it was seismic. *But I will have collateral.*

And then he sprang.

Desdemona was surrounded. Nowhere to hide or run. The Kobold King was everywhere. Quicksilver and white fire and thallium flame. His mouth stretched open—wide enough to swallow her head. From the rippling mirror of his face snaked a batrachian green tongue. It extended out and out, the forked tip swiping down and gluing itself to her forehead.

She tried to scream, but her throat refused to obey. It was like drowning in the brilliant acid undertow of the Mirradarra Doorway all over again. And then that thin green tongue was moving, flickering, flicking: a sinuous whiplash against her forehead. Desdemona felt the shape of a figure eight emerge from her flesh like scar tissue. And then the Kobold King withdrew his tongue.

Standing a little back from her, he opened his hand again. The crumpled newsprint blossomed from his palm like a burning rose, still feeding on the kindling of those thirty-six names. He brought his hand to Desdemona's forehead and pressed one finger to the topmost oval of the figure eight his tongue had just described. The flame swirling on his palm leapt up to swarm his knuckles, and from there separated into thirty-six tiny tongues of fire, each enclosing a single name that marched like an ant across the bridge of his finger and onto Desdemona's forehead.

Her eyes crossing to focus on them, Desdemona moaned as these charred granules burrowed tick-like into her skin, filling the top bubble of the figure eight on her forehead like the upper bulb of an hourglass. Her whole brow felt on fire. Unbearably *full*. She could see them all so clearly, the miners whose names she carried, as if they stood before her, their faces black with coal dust, their eyes like lamps . . .

The moment the Kobold King released her, Desdemona clawed her face. But there was nothing there to scrape away. Her forehead was round and smooth beneath her fingers. Otter-sleek, otter-soft. But her senses were lying—they had to be!—for when she dropped her hands to her sides, she could still feel the figure eight protruding from her forehead like a feverish tumor.

"What have you done?" Desdemona scratched the mark, scrubbed it, tried to rub it out. Nothing. There was nothing there. "What have you done to me?"

I have accepted your barter. Now hear my terms.

Her fingers froze mid-scratch. "Terms?"

You will rescue my daughter from durance vile before the hourglass on your forehead empties. If you do, those thirty-six lives you seek are yours. You may return with them to Athe, where they will live again under the sun.

But, if you do not . . .

Desdemona's eyes widened. Her tails stiffened. Collateral. Hadn't he said something about collateral, right before he . . . ?

If you do not, the Kobold King continued, *thirty-six hounds will harry the one you love most through the halls of Breakers Beyond. When they catch her—and they will catch her—they will tear her into thirty-six suppers. She will die, and in eating her flesh those hounds will become my gob-linkin in true; they will never return home, and you shall sink down to the seven hells below, fodder for whatever there will feed on you. This is the price of your failure.*

A suck of silver light.

An abrupt lack of wind.

A whisper:

Do not fail me, Tattercoats.

And he was gone.

Alone once more in that vacuum of vanished bright-ness, Desdemona shivered—great, juddering shudders that started at her center and shook through her body like shock waves. The sigil on her forehead let out a high, sweet *ping*! Somewhere, just inside her skin, the finest, minutest trickle of glowing green letters began to tumble from her hairline down the bridge of her nose, sifting into the lower bulb of the hourglass.

Time. Desdemona did not know how much she had, but she knew it was running out.

And then, out of a darkness that was gradually becom-ing gray scale again as her night vision adjusted, so ten-tatively that the sound did not even startle her, a voice called her name.

"Desdemona?"

Desdemona closed her eyes.

"Desi? Is that you?"

10

THE DAMSEL HOLE

DESDEMONA TURNED, heartsick and snowdrift-slow, and saw Chaz.

Or rather, she saw a woman who looked like Chaz.

Or rather, she saw Chaz . . . who was a woman.

Or rather—and the certainty of her next thought swept a wave of gooseflesh through Desdemona's body that made her fur stand on end—she saw Chaz, who had always been a woman, and whose outward appearance now matched that truth. The Kobold King, as he had done for Desdemona, had given Chaz a new skin. One that she had chosen for herself, her heart's desire—the skin she should have been born with.

The curves filling out her dress needed no structural support to shape them, any more than the red curls uncoiling past her waist in luxurious disarray belonged to a wig. The long angles of her jaw had filled out and rounded, and the cartilaginous prominence of the larynx that Chaz had always despised was . . . gone. She was dressed in the same high-necked metallic ivory caftan she had been wearing when she and Desdemona drank champagne together in the billiards room at Breaker House. Perhaps this *was* the billiards room, only two worlds down, and Chaz had never left it. Just fallen through.

"Look at you," Chaz whispered, her eyes round and shocked like a coconut's. "What happened to you?"

Desdemona was heartened that Chaz recognized her at all, this strange beast she had become, with too many claws, too many fangs, too many patchwork parts to name. Pleased, her tails began wagging.

"I am a Thousandfurs," she said, and for the first time since waking in this world, Desdemona smiled.

Something in that smile, fangs and all, must have convinced Chaz that it was all right to burst into tears and throw herself into Desdemona's arms. The initial impact knocked Desdemona back a few steps, but then she planted her feet firmly and resigned herself to Chaz's scolding, tear-scalded embrace.

"I thought I'd never find you. You *left* me! I came all this way—*and you were not here!*"

Chaz's usually impeccable maquillage looked like a massacre: her bloodshot eyes were ringed like a meerkat's mask, there was mud crack in her rice powder, and a smear of streaky scarlet trailing from one corner of her swollen mouth like blood spatter at a crime scene. She was still crying, but more quietly now, without full awareness but with immaculate self-possession, like a piano prelude meant to imitate rainfall.

Tears had always made Desdemona cross.

"Dry up, Chaz! I've already drowned once today!"

But she clung to her friend in turn, holding her ferociously close with both arms and several of her tails. "I know I'm late," she admitted. "I was waylaid. I'm sorry you were frightened, but I'm here now. And we haven't much time."

Time. Her forehead throbbed in reminder. Her mind roared with names and flames and time dripping away, and she looked at her friend, who was dearer to her than anyone, and who must not—who must never, *never*—flee for her life through these cavernous halls with hounds baying at her heels. And Desdemona realized for the first time that she was seeing Chaz, not in night-sight shades of gray, but in color. The light source, she discovered in short order, came from something Chaz carried balled up in her hand.

"What's that you're holding, Chazzy?" Desdemona asked. "Is it . . . *sizzling*?"

"This?" Chaz looked down, laughed in surprise, and shrugged her sequined shoulders. "I forgot I had it! Some old hat, I think? I found it by the river. It was sort of sparkling, so I picked it up. I was using it as a kind of lantern, because I couldn't see a damned thing down here, but then it began tugging me—a little at first, then quite insistently—and led me here to you."

"Oh, it did, did it?" Grimly, Desdemona snatched Farklewhit's bedraggled cap from Chaz's hand. The crackling pom-pom at the tip of its trailing end made a burping noise and blushed a rosy pink. Holding it by one end like a limp squirrel, Desdemona plunged her hand into the depths of the hat—her arm sinking elbow-deep—and pulled as hard as she could.

Like a harlequin on a hidden spring, out snapped the Umber Farklewhit, pink lace apron and all.

"Hello, Tattercoats!" He looked her up and down admiringly. "You're looking fine as a barrel of weasels in a rabbit warren. Much improved! Ready to take on the Valwode? If any gentry trap tries to snap you up now, you just scratch right back! You've the claws for it now."

Desdemona pounced. "You!"

Or tried to pounce. Farklewhit snatched her out of the air and swung her around in a kind of do-si-do.

"SPLISH she falls and SPLOSH she floats!" he shouted. "And SPLASH, we have a Tattercoats!"

The rankness of his woolly body washed up her nose, and she did not know if it was this or the spinning that dizzied her. It was as if a secondary sense of smell suddenly kicked in, much more complex than her human one, more curious and discerning but with a remarkable lack of judgment. Her nostrils quivered and flared, analyzing Farklewhit's particular stench, imprinting on it, and something inside her, some instinct to explore awakened, urging her to pursue that scent, burrow into it, mingle with it, start to lick . . .

Farklewhit grinned with manic winsomeness and released her from his hold mid-spin, sending her crashing into Chaz.

"Introduce me to your friend?" he asked. "At least, I assume you two know each other, cozy as you are. Is she one of your salacious sopranos?" He waggled his eyebrows.

"No—ew!" said Desdemona. "This is my sister, Chaz."

"Sisters? I'd never have guessed!" Farklewhit curtsied to Chaz, who gasped at the shameless display beneath his apron. "Not that you aren't *very* pretty," he complimented her. "But she"—with a jerk of his thumb toward Desdemona—"is more my type."

Chaz's eyes, if it were possible, went even rounder and wider. The perplexed crinkle on her brow marked the halfway point between a nervous giggle and running off screaming into the darkness. Desdemona barged between them, barking, "Less talk, more momentum!" She pointed all nine of her tails right at Farklewhit's V-shaped nose. "Are you here to help, Nanny? If not, leave. If so, stay close. No more disappearing into your hat—or it'll be Farklemutton for supper, my loves."

"Oh"—and Farklewhit curtsied like a wanton wedding cake, wool-flavored, with lacy pink fondant—"I'm here for the duration, Tattercoats!"

His tail, a pudgy, stubby thing with a tufted end, began to wag. Several of Desdemona's enthusiastically followed suit until she slapped them back behind her.

"Very well." She rubbed the back of her ruffled neck. "Follow me. Coming, Chazzy?"

She held out her hand. Chaz caught it up almost violently, like a mountaineer gripping a lifeline before going over the side of a cliff. She put her mouth to Desdemona's ear and whispered, "Desdemona. What is *that*?" with a swift sideways glance at Farklewhit.

"He's . . . the goblin ambassador to the Valwode."

"He's *wha* . . ." Chaz stopped and shook her head. "And . . ." She paused again and rubbed her smooth throat. "How do you know him?"

"He saved my life."

"Oh!" Chaz's grip tightened like a vice. Her breath blew out another "Oh," this one much more quiet.

"Well," she said in a stronger voice, "I'm here now, too. To—to have your back. I'll help keep you safe. Me and that . . . Farklewhatever."

"Farklewhit," Farklewhit said helpfully. He seemed to be holding himself very still, allowing Chaz time to adjust.

"Farklewhit," Chaz repeated, daring another glance his way. She scooted a little closer to Desdemona but included both of them when she spoke next. "What happens now? My head—the champagne—and then waking up here. Like, like this. Everything feels a bit muzzy and achy, and I don't remember ..." She squeezed her eyes shut. "We came here," she recalled slowly, "because of the Merula Colliery disaster." Her eyes flew open to stare at Desdemona. "You said there were men down here. You were going to find them. And something ... something about the woman in the painting? Howell's painting."

"Susurra the Night Hag," Desdemona prompted.

"Susurra." Chaz's tear-ravaged face softened, glowed. "Susurra, yes."

A tremor passed through her body. She lifted to her tiptoes, as if to reach something tantalizing yet unachievable. Almost instantly, she fell back onto her soles, but also lightly, as if her ankles had suddenly sprouted fluttering white moth wings. "We have to ... to save her?"

"That's right," Desdemona affirmed. "Before you found me, I made a bargain with the Kobold King to trade his lost daughter for my miners. A bad bargain, maybe. Kantzaros gave me a time limit, and . . ." Her forehead itched. Burned.

As confidently as she could, she finished, "And so, we have to get going! Onward!"

With that, still holding Chaz's hand, she set off purposefully in the one direction that seemed to angle uphill. Whether uphill also indicated up-world, Desdemona had no idea. Chaz, stately in her heels, trotted to keep abreast with her.

"Onward?" Chaz called. "*That's* your plan?"

As plans went, "onward" was utter bunkum, and they both knew it. So did Farklewhit, who quickly caught up with the two of them. Taking Desdemona's other hand, he swung it to and fro like a child and with great interest inquired, "So you've discovered the location of Susurra's prison, then?"

Desdemona swallowed but said nothing. She quickened her pace. Chaz, reading that balky silence like a dog-eared book, groaned, "Oh, Desi! Just tell the truth. Don't lead us on a jackalope chase through the darkness. I can hardly see a thing except Farterwhit's—"

"Farklewhit," said Farklewhit.

"—Farklewhit's hat. I swear, I've never felt more in sympathy with a planchette on a spirit board!"

Time dribbled down Desdemona's brow. Chaz's life, running down the hourglass. Oily sweat slicked her furs to her body. How crowded and watchful the vast darkness seemed suddenly to be, as if hundreds of pairs of eyes peeked out from behind the spiraling pillars of the speleothems, which themselves seemed to grow less sessile, more watchful, the moment she began to pay them attention. Desdemona's knees locked, buckled. She stumbled to a halt.

"Farklewhit—Chaz is right," she blurted in confession. "I don't . . . I don't have a plan! I don't know how to find Susurra. We need to go back to the Valwode—but I don't know how to get there!"

"In fact . . ." Farklewhit bounded up to her side. ". . . getting to the Valwode is simple from here—easy as rapping on a wall!" He winked at her. "Really, Tattercoats—all you had to do was *ask*!"

"Farklewhit!" Chaz shouted.

"*Nanny!*" Desdemona growled at the same time. "You could have just *said*."

"Me? I can't help my nature!"

As he spoke, he was trotting over to a particularly immense stalagmite, where he stopped and gave the stone three smart knocks. A block of rock shifted, revealing a narrow stair winding up. Turning back to them, Farklewhit grinned.

"You see? In Day Breakers, the walls only open at midnight. In Dark Breakers, it's never midnight but at old doorways like the Mirradarra. Well! Here in Breakers Beyond, it's always midnight—and the doors are always open!"

~

They climbed so long that Desdemona began entertaining the idea of Farklemutton far more seriously. Her stomach complained so loudly that she wondered if she had more than one of them now, like her eyelids and her ears. They climbed until even Chaz surrendered and removed her heels, leaving them forlorn on the steps. Farklewhit just kept bustling on ahead of them, indefatigably cheerful, never once looking back, even when Desdemona's stomach let out a sound like a foghorn.

He did, however, exclaim, "Ah, borborygmus!" with a joyous little wiggle. "No sound sweeter!"

Desdemona's eyes fastened on his rump. For some inexplicable reason she began salivating. His unfathomable rankness continued to confuse her nose. She did not know if she wanted to tear into him or just take him.

"We used to call her Bubbleguts when we were kids," Chaz offered breathlessly from the rear.

"Chaz!" Desdemona considered giving her friend a swift kick back down the stairs.

"Bubbleguts!" Farklewhit fairly vibrated with glee.

Now he began hopping up the steps two at a time, his black hooves clacking like glass against the stones as he chanted:

"Tattercoats Bubbleguts, Nine-Tails True
Climbs through the worlds with comrades two
Claws on her fingers and points in her smile
Rescues our princess from durance vile!"

At couplet's end, he gave one last great hop, clearing a dozen steps at least, and disappeared into the darkness beyond.

"Nanny?" Desdemona and Chaz called at the same time.

"Up here!" Farklewhit's face appeared. "We made it!" He looked over his shoulder. "We appear to have emerged in one of the sub-basements of Dark Breakers."

"You sound excessively pleased," Desdemona observed sourly, dragging herself up the last few steps. She was hungry. Her throat was dry. Her calves and thighs ached from climbing. All those infinite stairs to end up in this not very prepossessing room, with no visible way out.

Farklewhit rubbed his hands together. "Oh, I am, Tattercoats! I am!"

"Why?" asked Chaz, finally flinging herself to the floor like a beached mermaid.

"Because," Farklewhit explained, moving deeper into

the room, the light of his hat bobbing along with him, "I've spent the last two years in Dark Breakers. I've been through the whole of it, tower to cellar. I've seen every room: the ones that swap places when you're not looking, the ones that grant your every desire to keep you in them, the ones that only appear while the stars align just so. I've torn this place apart looking for my Susurra—*but I have never been here.*"

There was no doubt they were in the Valwode; even what appeared to be a sub-basement managed, despite having no visible light fixtures or braziers to illuminate it, to glow with that gallimaufry of moonlight, twilight, and predatory flower-light that pervaded this side of the Veil. Desdemona glared about at dusty barrels of dark gentry wines, casks of ciders exuding the smell of apples and honey, heaps of forgotten hand spindles and spinning wheels (the shafts of the former sharp as poniards; the latter with rovings of straw still dangling from slender lead yarns of golden floss), baskets of jeweled fruit from the orchard, broken thrones, shattered birdcages.

And shelves and shelves of bone bells.

"Now what?" she asked.

Farklewhit popped up right behind her. "*Your* task! You tell me!"

Desdemona whirled to glower at him, but he merely gazed at her with the absolute trust of a dog with a sausage on his nose. Groaning, she ground her palms against her eyes until the pressure exploded into phosphenes. "How should I know? I've never been here either!"

From where she sprawled on the floor, Chaz flung out her hand to encircle Desdemona's ankle and squeeze lightly. It would have been a comforting gesture, except that Chaz dug her nails in, just enough to irritate her. Desdemona grunted and shook off her friend's grip. She also dropped her hands from her face and stood up a little straighter.

Calm as a nanny nurturing a malignity of goblin moppets, Farklewhit said, "Tattercoats. There are three reasons why you will—why you *must*—succeed where all others, including myself, have failed. One: Nyx herself assigned you this task. You wanted something; she told you how to get it. That's better than a blessing. Two"—Farklewhit's eyes shifted to Chaz—"you are sufficiently motivated. From what I know of the Mannerings, sufficient motivation can move them to move mountains—with or without dynamite. Three: our lost Susurra is hidden in the house where you grew up. Surely you know all the hidey-holes of Breaker House?"

"Not *Dark* Breakers," Desdemona protested. "I lived in, in . . . *Day* Breakers. And only for the summer months. I hardly . . ."

"Stop whining, Desi!" Chaz's fingernails dug in again as she hauled herself up to a sitting position. "Think! Hiding places! How many times in our lives did you thrust me into a closet—or a wardrobe, or a kitchen cupboard—and lock me in and leave me there for hours? What you don't know about imprisoning princesses who've displeased you isn't worth knowing."

Desdemona realized she was smiling. "The butler's pantry?"

Chaz dusted smut off her sequins, shuddering delicately. "Don't remind me. That place didn't even have the affordances of liquor. Just all your mother's old china and silver. I was ready to drink metal polish by the time you let me out."

Farklewhit kicked a spindle across the room like a pigskin ball, startling both of them. "No, no, *no*! The oubliette where Nyx consigned Susurra won't take its mortal parallel in a butler's pantry or an old wardrobe. It will be in some *forgotten* spot. It cannot," he explicated, "have any other function but to contain something *secret*." And though he sounded calm and reasonable, Desdemona saw the ardent hope flash across his face and was almost afraid of it. "Do you know of a place like this, Tattercoats?"

Stiffening her resolve, Desdemona settled to the work of serious thought. "H.H.'s safe?"

"The one in his office?" asked Chaz. "Everyone knows where that is."

"But they don't all know the combo." And after all, Desdemona thought, it's where H.H. keeps the contract.

Chaz suggested, "What about the storage attics?"

Desdemona shook her head. "Servants live up there. Not a private corner to kiss in."

Plopping herself atop a barrel of wine, sparkling skirts spread, elbows on knees, Chaz said, "Wine cellar?" and peered around. "A cellar's sort of like a sub-basement, right? And if—like Farklewhit suggested—we emerged *here* for a reason, maybe . . . ?" she trailed off.

Desdemona snorted. "Chaz—you know the traffic in our wine cellar rivals Seafall's rush hour! We can't sneak out a bottle of sherry without three sommeliers popping out of thin air to lecture us on its provenance. It would be the absolute *worst* place to hide something. Except, of course, that time when Mother hid an entire . . ."

She stopped. She had spoken before the memory completed itself. But now, remembering, Desdemona's tongue curled against the roof of her mouth, and she stared into the murk-light of Dark Breakers' deepest chamber, seeing a different cellar out of much, much younger eyes.

"Hid wha—" Chaz began, but Farklewhit said sharply, "Hush! Let her think!"

But nothing Chaz said could distract Desdemona from the memories now crowding in. Until her fifth birthday (in which landmark year the women of Southern Leressa and the Federation Islands finally won the right to vote), Tracy Mannering, whose maternal instincts in no way conflicted with her political leanings, would strap her young daughter—gussied up in cuirass and bronze galea for the occasion—into a wagon disguised as a float and give her a FORWARD OUT OF DARKNESS sign to carry. Together, they would attend events like the All Women of Seafall suffrage parades, which had been organized, of course, by Tracy Mannering and her sister-in-law, Audrey. Sometimes they would go to secret meetings, where women gathered to discuss strategy and practice self-defense. And the place where Tracy and Audrey *held* those meetings was . . .

Desdemona shouted, "The Damsel Hole!"

Chaz blinked. "The . . . excuse me?"

The bulbous itch on the bridge of her nose blazed joyously. Desdemona rubbed it and paced, paced and rubbed, and remembered. "Mother's hidden room! In our cellar at Breaker House. For the suffragists. They called it the Damsel Hole. It was"—she grinned suddenly—"one of Aunt Audrey's little vulgarities."

Farklewhit squatted down at Chaz's side, watching with silent intensity as Desdemona strode back and forth. "Twenty-something years ago"—the words were tumbling out of her now—"before we got the vote, the political temper of the city was really heating up. The women of Seafall were given a curfew. It became illegal for them to meet publicly in numbers greater than three. So Mother and Aunt Audrey walled off part of the wine cellar at Breaker House. It was our summer cottage, shuttered all the rest of the year, so they came down in winter without H.H. knowing and brought in all-female contractors from the mainland. They excavated a tunnel to a secret entrance some distance from the house, so that women from the suffrage movement could enter and leave without being seen. Anyway—after winning the franchise, Mother walled off the room again and paved over the tunnel's entrance. She built a pagoda there, planted a few rosebushes. *A secret place should be kept a secret*, she said, *till it's needed again*. And, according to Mother, it will *always* be needed again."

Desdemona realized she had stopped pacing, right in front of a moonstone-paneled wall. It was half-obscured behind a stack of casks, and she stared at it almost without seeing it. "Mother ordered me to lock it up, too—in my head. For *women only*, she said. So I'd forgot about it. Until now."

Farklewhit sprang from the floor, amber eyes alight, and scooped her into a rib-cracking embrace, singing out, "That's it!!"

He squeezed her until she squeaked. "I knew it!" he said. "I knew you'd have it tucked away in you somewhere. That's my good monster!"

Desdemona grinned crookedly, sagging into his radiant stench. "I am my mother's daughter," she said softly, and wished—how she wished!—it were really true.

Farklewhit barked a happy shout of laughter. "That you are!"

Shaking her to and fro, he twirled her around and around until she laughed and shouted, "What next, Nanny?"

"Take us to her, Tattercoats. Bring us to Susurra!"

Desdemona was so giddy by then that she grabbed Farklewhit by his curly horns, reared back, and smashed forward, ramming the hourglass on her forehead against his woolly pate.

The knock sent stars spinning through her skull. She reeled through the cosmos, through the forgotten detritus of uncounted gentry generations, and came up hard up against the blank, featureless wall. She set her hand upon its glassy surface . . .

And pushed right through.

11

DURANCE VILE

THE SECRET ROOM WAS small and round. At its center, dominating the space but for a thin circumference of walkway surrounding it, was a cage. Its bars grew down from the ceiling and pierced through the floor like the roots of an old iron tree. The iron looked out of place in the Valwode, cruel and dull, as if even the light feared to touch it. A rusty abscess burrowing into the beautiful dream.

Desdemona gripped her splitting skull and closed her eyes. Why had she butted Farklewhit's head like that? She had to swallow several mouthfuls of saliva before the nausea passed and she could see again.

The opaque outer walls of the oubliette, having thinned to mist when Desdemona passed through them, firmed up again after Chaz and Farklewhit tumbled into the room behind her. They jostled her throbbing skull with loud congratulations and crowded her with exultant embraces. Swallowing a surge of near-vomit, she shoved them away, and they went off laughing to examine the cage more closely. Desdemona crumpled against the smooth wall, head between her knees, and tried to breathe deeply.

She only looked up when she heard Farklewhit call out in a tender voice, "Surra-lurra? O my hagliest? My nursling? Wake thou, and speak to thine own Umber-sire."

Desdemona could see him standing on the far side of the cage, peering in. His eyes flashed between the bars, jeweled pools of fiery amber in the moon-cool room. After a long pause, something stirred within the cage. Thin as snakeskin tumbling over a stony plain, the answer came.

"Nanny?"

Farklewhit's sensitive lips trembled. He stepped closer to the cage, raising his hands, almost touching the iron bars. "It is I, my mandragora. And these two here, who helped me find you."

He nodded toward Desdemona through the bars. Desdemona thought she saw movement in the cage, something turning slowly to look at her.

"A Tattercoats came down-worlds to barter for her heart's desire—and you were your fond father's fee. He has branded her brow, threatened those she held dear, and demanded her life in forfeit if she failed—but she performed her task beautifully." He pointed at Chaz. "This one's the beloved. The sacrifice, should we fail to ply you free."

"Poor maid," said the voice, and another slight, restless movement indicated that the speaker had turned toward Chaz. "How tender she is. How new."

Desdemona's eyes began to sort the shadows at the center of the cage into a heap of rags and spindly limbs. Susurra was sucked as deeply into herself—and as far from the iron bars—as goblinly possible. Two black-purple points, like the berries of a deadly nightshade, gleamed out from a face the color of lace left to molder on a tombstone. She was staring at Chaz.

"Would you be goblin meat, maid," she asked, "for my sake? *Flee!*"

"What are you talking about?" asked Chaz. "I'm not anyone's meat." Her back was to her best friend; Chaz could not see Desdemona flinch and stagger to her feet as she herself advanced toward the cage in a rustle of soiled glitter. Puddling down to the floor, Chaz pressed her face against the bars.

"Why do you look at me so kindly?" Susurra demanded in her desiccated voice. "I am nothing. I am finished."

"Princess, I came all this way," Chaz whispered across the malicious shadows that piled between herself and

Susurra. Her voice was so tender with pity that Desdemona almost did not recognize it. "Three nights ago—a lifetime ago—I saw your likeness in a painting. Ever since then, I have longed to help you. I, too, know what it's like to be"—she drew in an unsteady breath—"caged."

Susurra let out a soughing sob. "Free me! Free me, maid, I beg you! Or kill me before you leave again—for I cannot bear it!"

Chaz thrust an arm through the bars and reached out to her. "Princess . . . how long is it since you've been touched?"

"Years."

After a short hesitation, Susurra stretched out on her belly. Slowly, she began sliding herself, inch by agonizing inch, closer to the iron bars.

"Years since any touch or taste or kiss."

Her long, many-jointed fingers sidled up to Chaz's wrist, wrapping it once about, then twice—like, Desdemona thought, a parasitic vine.

"Years," said Susurra, "since I have sucked the fruit of the Ympsie tree, or drunk of hangman's dew, or licked the dwayberries our merry boys brought to market in their baskets of blue grave moss."

Bending her head, the goblin girl set her pallid cheek against Chaz's palm. The dark lights in her eyes blinked out as her exhausted lids fell.

"Beloved maid," she whispered, "I beg you. Pass me some blade, some broken mirror. Open your kindly veins for my cup—a very little will do. Let me drink the iron in your blood and die of it. Oh, if Nyx had been kind, she would have killed me quickly! But she left me here—and forgot me!"

Farklewhit made a noise of distress. Tears were rolling down Chaz's face. Only Desdemona, trying to hold her splitting head together and keep her nausea at bay, felt nothing but a sick impatience.

"Oh, my princess!" said Chaz. "We will free you and be rid of this place. You will live—and thrive!—and spite those who would obliterate you. I know something of this, too. I'll help you." Casting a quick, scolding look over her shoulder, Chaz ordered Desdemona, "Don't lummox about like a knuckle-dragger! Unlock her cage!"

Desdemona opened her mouth to retort, but a searing pain scorched her brow and took all her breath with it. She whumphed instead.

"There is no door," Farklewhit said flatly. "I've been around the cage twice."

Susurra nestled deeper into Chaz's palm. Chaz reached her other arm through the bars to stroke her hair.

"There is no door," the goblin girl affirmed. "There is no key. There is no way out for you or me . . . my beloved."

Desdemona blinked, dizzy, as the scoring pain began to fade. Something was happening inside the cage. A series of slow, slender movements she could not quite parse. Until she could. Inspirited by Chaz's caresses, Susurra's hair had begun to stir. The long strands lifted themselves into the air like the legs of prodigious black widows stitched abdomen-first into the mushroom-sallow skin of Susurra's skull. Stiff, strange, and shiny black like Farklewhit's hooves, each separate strand was segmented and clawed, sensitive to the movements of its neighbors but acting of its own accord.

"Chaz," Desdemona warned apprehensively.

Chaz's glower of burning reproach was harsh enough to make Desdemona drive her thumbs under the ridge of her brow. She wished her fingers were either very hot knitting needles or sharpened icicles. On the floor, still stroking Susurra's sinister hair, Chaz started crooning to the Night Hag as if she happened to be a stray animal bedraggled by rain and wind.

"You poor thing. You poor, tired darling."

Susurra's unhappy yawn showed a glimpse of tiny, pointed teeth.

"Nyx caged me that I might learn to dream the Valwode strong," she confided in her iron-abraded voice. "But I could never dream here. Never sleep. Not once, with all this iron about me. No friends, no food, no night to shutter my eyes. For years. To be imprisoned, I know, was what I deserved for my act of treachery. But oh, I would have preferred death!"

"Hush! No more talk of death. Sleep now." Chaz set the fingertips of her free hand over Susurra's eyelids, like silk buttons on a butterfly's wings. "Dream that you wake free."

Susurra's breathing slowed and deepened. Soon, she was asleep.

The bridge of Desdemona's nose was flaring and pulsing like a terrible green coal. The top of her skull felt sawed off, empty. Time, time! She was almost out of it. But she could not think. She could barely see through the rain of infinitesimal scalpels lancing the whites of her eyeballs. Think! She had to *think*!

Farklewhit pounced. "Tattercoats!"

Desdemona yelped. Last she'd glimpsed him, Farklewhit had been prowling around the cage, examining it from all angles. Now, he was standing before her, crackling with fury.

"No door!" His shout penetrated her pain fog. "Seven hells swallow me! Did I come all this way under your hourglass just to stare at what I cannot touch?"

Desdemona shook her head, trying to free it from the thorn thicket growing out of her eye sockets.

"What do you mean there's no door?"

Farklewhit threw up his hairy arms. "What do you mean what do I mean? See for yourself: all bars, no door. All cage, no key. No window, no latch, no catch, no joint, no jamb, no ingress or egress. No hope. For any of us!"

"But . . ." Desdemona pointed. "There *is* a door!"

"What?" Farklewhit's arms fell. Very quietly he asked, "What did you say?"

"That door. *There.*"

It was right in front of them; Desdemona could see it more clearly than anything else through the green-edged aura of her migraine. The door was the shape of an hourglass, translucent. It had not been there until Chaz put Susurra to sleep, after adjuring her to dream herself free. Susurra, it seemed, was following orders.

Farklewhit turned to look and yelped. But Chaz, whose left arm had seemingly been bisected by a vitreous guillotine when the door appeared, only gasped softly. On the other side of the glass, her hand kept stroking Susurra's hair. The clear pane magnified and distorted Susurra's shape, bloating her like a river-bottom corpse, her hair an undulating forest of black waterweeds. Desdemona began to laugh. The sound came out in short, sharp screams.

"There! Now she's dreamed the key! The key is in the lock!"

But though it was Susurra who dreamed the door, it was still Nyx the Nightwalker's key. The bow was an elaborate twist of black iron, cold and deadly, and the shank, long as a shiv, was jammed up to its collar in the center of the hourglass. Farklewhit leapt at it, and when his fingers closed around the shank, he sighed in triumphant relief.

This immediately turned into a hiss of pain. His hand began to smoke. Green blood boiled from his cuticles. The woolly hair on his fingers blackened and curled off in singed crisps. Farklewhit roared in pain but kept his grip on the key, throwing his body's weight against the lock. But the key would not turn.

Finally, he wrenched away before the iron melted his hand right through, howling, "Nyx, you night worm! You slimy, daughter-stealing, double-crossing, clay-kissing traitor! Give me a key I can *turn*!" and hurled himself against the iron bars. Each time his body made impact, there was a clang like the inside of a cathedral bell, the smell of scorched mutton.

"Nanny!" Desdemona flattened herself against the bars in front of him, throwing her arms out. "Nanny, stop! Stop!"

Her outstretched fingers slicked the iron key. It was cold to the touch, slick from Farklewhit's greasy goblin blood, but it did not burn her.

Farklewhit wheeled away from her, burly arms blackened, broad chest smoking, looking for another opening in the cage. His pink lace apron was in tatters, his pelt matted, splattered with blood and fluid from burst blisters. At the sight of his wildness, Desdemona was crushed by the same pity she had seen on Chaz's face. She had never known anything like it. It felt like dying.

No. That was not precisely true, was it? She had felt this panicked sadness, this helplessness, twice before. The first time a few days ago at her mother's fund-raiser at the Seafall City Opera. And then again, when she read the headlines the next day. Terrible as this feeling was, it had brought her here, to this.

She said quietly, "Let me try, Nanny."

Whatever he heard in her voice stopped Farklewhit from throwing himself against the cage yet again. He sagged in front of Desdemona, eerily, mournfully calm.

"It's our last chance, Tattercoats. Your hourglass is almost . . ."

"I know." Desdemona turned to face the door. "But like you said—it's my task. Mrs. Howell sent *me*."

And closing her fingers around the key, she twisted it in the lock.

It was like trying to turn the world against its axis. Memory, all jumbled up with nightmare, crashed over her, like an iron tide dragging her from an iron shore: her mother at the head of a crowd of white-clad women, beating a policeman with her umbrella until he battered her to the sidewalk with his slapjack; her father, teeth clamped over his cigar, shouting into the telephone as black oil poured from his mouth; Salissay, on their stake-out of the ULE headquarters, sliding across the summer-sticky leather seats of the Model Noir to slip her tongue into Desdemona's mouth; the Phossy Gals dolled up in their evening gowns and diamonds, dying eyes defiant for the camera; a line of miners disappearing into the shaft station at Merula Colliery, the lamps on their helmets blazing like eyes; and last, Nyx the Nightwalker, sitting across the embroidered ultramarine expanse of their table at the Chiamberra, watching Desdemona.

Watching her. Right now. Weighing her, judging her: every tuft of fur, every tail, every tooth.

And then, almost imperceptibly, across time, across worlds, staring directly into Desdemona's eyes, Nyx nodded.

The world turned against its axis.

The iron key turned in its invisible lock.

The hourglass on Desdemona's forehead tipped, upended, like a decanter knocked on its side by careless revelers. The desperate pressure of those green-glowing names burst into the lightness of wings.

And the cage, shrieking, fell to dust.

12

HAG OF NIGHT

"SUSURRA!"

"Susurra's back!"

"The Night Hag has returned!"

The cage had disappeared and the secret oubliette with it, silicate walls atomizing into mists. When the mists had cleared, both from Desdemona's eyes and from inside her head, she saw that the four of them were standing, not in the forgotten sub-cellar of Dark Breakers, but in the royal courtroom. Right in the writhe of a riot.

The Gentry Sovereign sat on its silver-sickle throne as if trying not to sink into its hundred welcoming razors. Its hands were clenched whitely on its knees, two great golden cuffs with emeralds the size of alligator eggs clamping its wrists like shackles. If statues could sweat, Desdemona imagined the Gentry Sovereign would be perspiring like a prisoner put to the question. At the foot of the dais, the gentry mob was shouting, jostling for a better look at Susurra and her rescuers. Thankfully, they did not collectively swarm the little group, which had emerged—out of the floor? Out of the very air itself?—on the wide bottom step of the dais, where they hunkered down in a protective huddle, Susurra at their center. This was too near the Gentry Sovereign for its subjects, even riled as they were, to dare venture.

But they wailed. They screamed. They reached for her.

"Nyx's heir!"

"The Dreamer!"

"Susurra, save us! Save us!"

Objects rocketed overhead and splatted down on the platform above them—nothing that could hurt or harm the Gentry Sovereign; its subjects were not yet so far gone as to risk their own lives like that—but globs of refuse, raining down. Mostly they were soft, rotted things like the faceted fruit of the orchard, jewels melting to slime; a spotted salmon wheezing dire prophecies as it drowned in air; wailing mandrake rootlings, bleeding from mouths and eyes; small winged bodies, limp and broken; more, so much more, all dead or dying, evidence of the Valwode failing, of the senescing dream. Some of the mess fell at the Gentry Sovereign's feet. Most slapped its sculpted chest and chiseled face, dripping down to mound on the green velvet and yellow satin of its robes. One tiny corpse was caught on the tines of the Antler Crown, where it slumped like a convict on a pike amidst the ivy leaves and honeysuckle entwined there.

"Alban Idris! Abdicate now!"

"We don't want you! We don't need you!"

"Susurra has returned!"

Desdemona covered her head and ducked an ill-lobbed papery meat-corpse just in time. But the Gentry Sovereign, on whom several simultaneous missiles actually made impact, did not so much as twitch a toe. If it did, Desdemona guessed that its older, scarier, brutal-looking policemen siblings would unsheathe their edged weapons and make short work of turning the royal court-room into an abattoir. Cold fury rose off their bodies, but they grimly held their positions, their dank chill like something seeping up from sinkholes in the earth.

"Des!" Chaz whispered. "Where's the exit?" She was hunched under Farklewhit's protective arm, cradling Susurra close to her chest. The goblin girl was still asleep, face buried in Chaz's neck. Desdemona was anxious about this instantaneous intimacy; Elliot Howell's paint-ing had hinted at Susurra's profusion of piranha teeth, and right now they were all too close to Chaz's veins.

"I don't think we're getting out of this," she answered, "until Alban Idris gives us leave."

This was something she thought unlikelier by the minute, as the calls for abdication and Susurra's corona-tion swelled to an ecstatic shouting, an orchestral chorus of song. There was a movement like a great wave when, as one body, all the gentry in the room surged forward.

At last the Gentry Sovereign sprang from its throne.

"SILENCE!"

Silence exploded into the room like a bolide fireballing from the sky.

Silence and stillness.

Desdemona hardly dared breathe. Next to her, Chaz crushed Susurra closer, hiding her face in all that strange hair. Farklewhit was making low "whup whup whup whup" noises, like a goat preparing either to scream or fall down in an angry faint.

The only thing that moved at all was the Gentry Sovereign—except, alarmingly, for the black-lit eyes of its viciously still siblings, which tracked that magnificent figure as it brushed fish scales and gem rot from its robes, shook its massive head until the corpse impaled on the Antler Crown flew across the room, and walked away from its silver throne, down the steps of the dais. The gentry mob remained frozen in bewitched watchfulness.

Stepping quickly down the steps, the Gentry Sovereign bounded down the last three with arms outstretched, demanding, "Give the girl to us! She must be brought to safety. She is our last hope—but we fear she might become an unintended casualty of the violence about to break."

But Farklewhit interposed himself between Susurra and the Gentry Sovereign, lowering his head with its hard-curled ivory horns and whup-whup-whupping some more. "You're not touching her," he snarled. "She's *ours*. You want to tangle with me, Alban Idris? I'll ram you into the sixth hell, where demon queens chew up rocks like taffy candy!"

"Ambassador." The Gentry Sovereign passed a hand briefly over its flickering, wounded eyes. "Your princess is not safe here. None of you are. The egg of this world is cracked. The Valwode is running to yolk between our fingers. If we cannot patch it . . ."

In Chaz's arms, Susurra stirred.

As she did, so did the gentry court, despite their enchanted stupor. The moment she opened her eyes, the first of the gentry unfroze and immediately began to rush toward her.

One of the policemen, a red-caped giant with an unfinished-looking face and a green flash in its eyes, drew a saw-toothed crystal sword from the silver-wrought sheath on its back and began wading through paralyzed gentry, the impact of its body sending them spinning and colliding.

Desdemona was the final impediment in its path. She could not get out of the way fast enough; the giant all but bulled her to the floor, closing in quickly on the runner. But the Gentry Sovereign caught the down-swinging blade in its hand, shouting wrathfully, "Cease this!"

The giant protested, "Sibling, we cannot allow . . ."

Seizing this moment of distraction, the gentry runner—a creature whose top teeth had apparently never stopped growing, for they brushed his concave belly and had been carved and colored as elaborately as scrimshaw, except for the roots, which still sported an inch of canvas-blank enamel—ducked beneath the Gentry Sovereign's arm to fall at Chaz's feet. Reaching up to take hold of Susurra's ragged cobweb hem, he pleaded through his teeth, "O Night Hag! Save us! Save our world! Dream this dictatorship undone! Free us!"

Sleepily, Susurra blinked down at him. Just as sleepily, she turned her face away, smiling up into Chaz's eyes instead with those purple-green-gloss lips—just as Howell had painted them—the color of cobra lilies.

"I woke up free," she whispered, "with your hair warming me. The way I dreamed it." Swiftly kissing Chaz on the mouth, she ordered, "Set me down, beloved. I am ready."

Chaz did not obey right away. After her first astonishment at the kiss, she bent her head and returned it, as Desdemona—and all the gentry court—watched. Even when their lips parted, their gazes remained locked, a wordless kything passing between them, such as Desdemona and Chaz had shared from their earliest years of friendship. Jealousy and bewilderment burbled at the back of Desdemona's throat but did not quite evolve into a noise of protest.

Chaz released Susurra to the floor, and she floated down as if suspended on threads of gossamer, landing like a water strider on the surface of a pond and glancing idly around the courtroom. Her gaze fell on the Gentry Sovereign. Her eyes glinted with arachnoidal amusement as she took in its stained opulence, the golden shackles on its wrists, the golden torque upon its throat, and at that look Desdemona recalled that Susurra was the twelfth daughter of Erl-Lord Kalos Kantzaros, and that tricks and treachery flowed through the green goblin ichor of her veins.

"You," the Night Hag said to the Gentry Sovereign, "are wearing *my* crown."

13

THE THREE-PETALED VOW

FARKLEWHIT GRABBED DESDEMONA'S HAND, squeezing like he could wring wishes from her bones. Her nine tails drummed his backside in reply: some angrily, a few reassuringly, and one or two just enjoying the shape of his woolly round rump.

His own stumpy tail lifted like a pennant in a brisk wind and flapped to and fro. He whispered excitedly, "She's getting stronger, Tattercoats! Ah! That blush like bug-guts upon her cheek! How her hairlegs shine, how keenly they click! My Susurra!"

What Desdemona perceived was that the longer Susurra stood there, hand in tender hand with Chaz, locked in death-by-staring combat with the Gentry Sovereign, the more substantial she seemed. She began to elongate like a shadow by moonlight until she was as stretched-tall as Alban Idris itself. Her cobwebby clothes were weaving themselves new lengths of silk, gray and gray and gray, billowing down her body in a heavy pyroclastic flow, heaping the moonstone tiles around her feet in piles of ash and folds of smoke.

At first the Gentry Sovereign only stared, stony-faced as the statue it once had been. Then—to Desdemona's amazement—it broke into one of its childlike, heart-breaking smiles.

"Oh! *That* is what it means to dream the world anew! Teach us, Lady of the Deep! Teach us to dream! We beg you!"

And it knelt at her feet.

"No!" The long-toothed gentry wailed. He who had run to Susurra's skirts now shrank behind them, hiding from the genuflecting ruler. "It is an abomination!" he moaned from concealment. "It is not one of us! It is not gentry! Even its human maker found it monstrous—he wished to smash that whole sinister race. O, Night Hag," he begged. "Dream those things destroyed. Release us from their thrall!"

Susurra did not spare the whingeing thing or its scrimshawed buckteeth a single glance, nor the rest of the gentry court either, however eagerly they took up his thread. A wave of movement rippled through the court-room as they pressed closer, adjuring her in a hundred voices to dream the living statues *undone*, to return full vigor to the Valwode.

The only perturbation she betrayed was the tightening

of her fingers upon Chaz's knuckles. But when the crush of gentry came too close for her comfort, she tossed her head. Her strange hair flailed out, warning whoever stood too close to *get back*, and she flashed a fanged smile, laughing at them all, "Who are *you* to make demands of *me*?"

"We are your subjects!" one of the green-skinned Bog Sisters answered, her hand on the hilt of her stone sword.

Susurra stopped laughing. She glared about with eyes like claws. "I am no gentry. I am koboldkin, born to the Bone Kingdom. I would be no temperate or solicitous ruler to you—not like this colossus who kneels before me, begging a better way to dream your world. See how it sets its hand beneath my foot? It does this for *you*. And yet you spurn its gentleness."

Her glance fell momentarily upon a single upturned face, a rapturous pair of blue eyes.

"All *I* know of gentleness," Susurra whispered, "I learned today."

Slipping her hand free of Chaz's grip, she leaped lightly into the air, like a spider leaps to the wind, and landed upon the Gentry Sovereign's bowed shoulders. It stayed perfectly still for her, surrendering to her wordless demand, content to be nothing more than a marble platform for her speeches.

"I am not here to bend my dreams to your whim!"

Susurra shouted to the courtroom scornfully. "If I dream the Valwode strong again, it shall run on the engine of *my* desire. Do you find the Veil Between Worlds a parlous place to live now? Wait till I have dwelled upon it! Darker than my own despair will my meditations turn your twilight. Reckless with traps and tricks, potholed with pitfalls into my father's world—whence monsters shall arise to romp amongst us! How melting-sweet you gentry waifs will taste upon our tongues. How you will crackle in our gnashing teeth. Are you *certain*," she pressed the recoiling royal court, "that you wish your perfect guardians"—and here she ran sensuous hands over the polished racks of the Antler Crown rising before her like a coppice—"*gone*?"

Silence.

"I thought not."

Towering above that fearful quiet, Susurra suddenly looked disoriented. Shadows shifted across her unpredictable face and then parted to reveal a lost, terrified thing, who stared into the tangle of antlers in her hands like a cage that would kill her to touch it. Throwing back her head, she began to shriek: a high, breathless, helpless noise, like a small creature being snatched up by a punishing pair of talons. She fell into the tines of the Antler Crown in a sobbing half faint. Hung there, moaning.

Farklewhit and Chaz rushed to help her. But the Gentry Sovereign was the first to untangle her, easing her off its shoulders, cuddling her to its massive, pale chest and crooning in a lullaby voice, low as an outgoing tide, "We did search for you, Lady of the Deep, we swear it. Ourself and the ambassador, and our siblings, too. Every hour—dusk till dusk till dusk—we looked in vain. He, frantic to find you. We, no less than he. But how can we ask anything of you now, when everything was taken from you? You have forgotten what it is to have plenty. What would you have of us? We will give you anything."

Susurra stirred. "Anything?"

"Anything," the Gentry Sovereign affirmed. "Except"—with a hint of regret—"the death of the Valwode. It was ceded us by Nyx the Nightwalker, to protect and keep as best as we were able. Alas," it sighed, "that we have done so badly against our yearning."

Reaching out for Chaz, who had taken one of her trembling hands, Susurra whimpered, "Beloved!"

Her hair extended in the other direction, twining itself around Farklewhit's neck. "Nanny! Help me!"

Eventually, in the cradle of all their arms, her sobs became hiccups, became sighs. With her breathing tranquil again, Susurra lifted her face to meet the concerned regard of the Gentry Sovereign. Green tracks stained her silver-green face, and her mouth was a woeful bent bow. "I see now why Auntie Nyx chose you," she said with great solemnity. "But, Majesty, it was all for naught."

Her head falling limply to its chest, the creeping feelers of her black hair loosened their stranglehold on Farklewhit to tiptoe up the sinewy white stalk of the Gentry Sovereign's neck. "You are far too soft to rule this fickle and capricious race," she told it wearily, "though you are made of stone. And I, though smoke, am far too hard."

The Gentry Sovereign bowed its head. "And so the Valwode is doomed."

Chaz, at Desdemona's side, opened her mouth. Paused as she considered the consequences of her words. Then drew a deep breath anyway, and with a brave and unwavering brightness, said, "But there's your solution!"

Susurra and the Gentry Sovereign turned to look at her.

Farklewhit, too.

The whole gentry court, too.

"What a pair you'd make!" Chaz said, as if explaining the obvious. "Mrs. Howell . . ." She cleared her throat. "Queen Nyx, that is, who was . . . must have thought that the two of you, together, would be . . . would be able to find the perfect, er, *composition*. Not a *tranquil* or symmetrical one, precisely . . . But a new kind of . . . art."

Her face began to shine as she warmed to one of her favorite subjects. "Where I come from, Seafall, Queen

Nyx's husband is a master artist. Rarely in the art world, in the city or abroad, do we see such subtleties of asymmetry as can be found in an Elliot Howell painting. Only someone who truly understands *balance* can so exquisitely manufacture its opposite. Such lively uneasiness of angle and echo, of shape, shadow, tone, such repetition of pattern, intersection of line! The careful observer can scarcely tear her eyes away. And—and—" Chaz hesitated, trying to tie her thoughts together. "Just as Howell's *art* embodies a powerful asymmetry"—her smile trembled—"I believe that Nyx's last and greatest dream for the Valwode—as odd, as *unlikely*, as it may seem—is manifest in you. Both of you. *Together.*"

Desdemona had known Chaz most of her life. Chaz could drop the monetary equivalent of a postsecondary education on a single piece of art, only to lock it up straightaway in a climate-controlled room where nobody else would ever see it—except, perhaps, her most intimate friends, and only when she was ludicrously inebriated. Art was Chaz's lifetime's obsession. One might even say religion. The expression on her face when she entered that sealed room and looked upon her collection could only be called worship. And it did not even *approach* the way Chaz looked at Susurra.

But Desdemona had just watched her friend essentially—and with a smile—*give Susurra away.*

A silent but intense sense of argument and agreement seemed to pass between the goblin princess and the Gentry Sovereign. Then they moved as one, Alban Idris setting Susurra back upon her feet with slow courtesy, she offering it in turn her long, long hand.

Bowing formally to kiss that green-veined inner wrist, the Gentry Sovereign promised, "Susurra the Night Hag, we will grant thee up to half our realm, and half the Antler Crown to set upon thy brow, if thou wouldst have us."

To the surprise of everyone, Susurra countered, "But I want only a third."

"A . . . third?" the Gentry Sovereign repeated.

"If, that is, you are willing to give the other third away."

"Ah."

The Gentry Sovereign turned to appraise Chaz, but it was Susurra who reached for her hand, taking it bashfully in her own and asking, "If you will . . . stay? With me? Beloved?"

"Oh!" Chaz touched her hair, her tattered dress, and then glanced at Desdemona, fear and longing in her face. Desdemona was frozen; she wanted to shake her head until her fur fell off, but she could not move. "It's just . . . But, I . . ."

"You are most welcome," the Gentry Sovereign assured her, possessing itself of her other hand. "The wisdom—not only to withstand art but to *interpret* it, and then to recognize asymmetry as a powerful beauty, is a rare commodity in any world. We must needs employ your expert eye: first, to bring the Valwode back into some stark balance; next, to help us tease out the gracious subtleties of uncertainty. And, for our own part . . ." The Gentry Sovereign's hand lifted, sifted through Chaz's curls. "We find your hair to be the brightest fire in the Valwode."

Chaz began to look a little drunk, as between them, Susurra and Alban Idris caressed her and whispered entreaties.

Desdemona turned to Farklewhit. "They want Chaz to stay? Forever?" For, possibly, eternity? Long past the time Desdemona was worm-dust in the Mannering Mausoleum? Chaz, the bright mortal bride to the immortal sovereigns of the Valwode? Was this what desolation felt like?

Farklewhit clapped his hands, delighted. "Ha! Yes! The Three-Petal Solution! That's the way of the World Flower! Why didn't I think of it? Nyx, you tricksy wight!" he cried to the ceiling. "Wicked sister, I could kiss you—though I curse your name!" With a caper of his shining hooves, he fluffed the remains of his apron. The gesture was not any more modest for the several significantly singed gaps in the pink lace—but that didn't faze

Farklewhit. Chattering at buffoonish speeds, he danced around the mutually betrotheds, speaking of wedding trousseaux and nuptial contracts, the guest list, the seating charts, goblin versus gentry versus human etiquette for the banquet, and asking, "Whatever will your father say, Susurra-li-urra?" and "Do you think we can get all of your sisters to attend?" and more along these lines until Susurra started shaking her head at him.

"No! No, Nanny, no, no, no! I want none of that! *You* are to perform the ceremony *now*! Bind us, Nanny. You are my Umber-sire. You speak with Da's voice."

Farklewhit stopped mid-caper. "Only at need."

"*I* need this. And the Valwode *needs* a dream, fleet and vast." Susurra wrapped Chaz close to her side. "I can dream nothing but nightmares till my place here is assured—and my beloved safe beside me." Her chin lifted. "Bind us *now*, Nanny. Split the Antler Crown amongst us three."

It did not escape Desdemona's notice that Susurra was also holding Alban Idris firmly by the hand as well. And it was *letting* her, smiling down with all apparent docility.

Three may rule the Valwode in *name*, but Desdemona rather thought she could hazard a guess as to which one of them would rule the *other* two.

But then, Chaz had always *liked* being ordered around. Right up until she didn't.

"Please!" Chaz broke away from her suitors. "Please, I need a minute. I need . . ."

And then she was standing in front of Desdemona, grabbing her hands and dragging her a little apart from the rest. Farklewhit stood guard in front of them, amiably whup-whup-whupping away any gentry busybody who sidled too near.

"What do you think?" Chaz whispered.

As Desdemona looked at her friend, a smile rose to her lips like the surface glitter of a lake, all while her heart dropped like a stone to the black, cold bottom. Already she could feel herself tucking the memory of Chaz away—this Chaz, as she was right now, truly happy for perhaps the first time since Desdemona had met her—Chaz, and her blazingly open smile. She would take the image down into the deep-lake darkness and bury it in the cool silt, preserving her memory like a rare wine cellared for the next generation.

"I think," Desdemona replied, squeezing Chaz's hands, "that this means no more stupid soup-and-fish suits for you."

Laughing, Chaz agreed, "No, never again!"

But still she clung to Desdemona's fingers. She shook her head, not in refusal or denial, but in happy disbelief. "How is this happening, Desi? How can this be possible?"

Desdemona shrugged, her smile twisting. "Because Susurra is dreaming it?"

"No." Chaz shook her head. "Susurra can change the world around me if she chooses, but she cannot compel my decisions. She would if she could!" She laughed. "I could see her trying. Actually, she's a bit like *you* when you want something, Desi. No." That little head shake again. "This? Right now? I think *I* might be dreaming it. The way they look at me? The way they see *me*? Desi—I've dreamed of *that* all my life."

And there it was. Chaz wasn't here to be convinced otherwise; she was here to be spurred onward. And Desdemona owed her that—for having known Chaz all her life but never truly having *seen* her. She knew her duty.

"You'd better hoof it, then," she advised.

"You'll stand as my witness," Chaz said, with a hint of anxiety, "or I swear I'll take one of your tails for my stole!"

Desdemona cheerfully flicked her the universal sign of ill will—hand up, knuckles out, first three fingers twisted together, indicating a mixed breeding from all three worlds—and spinning Chaz around to face her suitors, gave her a little push. Blushing like cotton candy caught in the act, Chaz joined Susurra and Alban Idris, holding out her hands to them. They reached for her, drawing her close again, and Chaz beaconed out a smile of such indelible elation that it lit the royal courtroom like the noontime sun of Athe.

Rubbing his hands together, Farklewhit came up behind Desdemona and clapped her on the back. "Well, if you're all sure, then—let us proceed!" And then there was no more time to dwell in melancholy—for he caught up Desdemona's elbow and galloped her up the steps to the dais while the others processed up behind them in a statelier manner. Desdemona laughed at the speed, but she did not stumble; her new body was too well balanced, with its sleek limbs and bare paws and all her tails helping. They attained the glimmering opal disk of the dais before the others did and took center stage, right in front of the silver sickle throne, which was terrifyingly large this close up.

Mouth close to her paired ears, Farklewhit ordered, "Stand just here, Tattercoats. You're the witness now."

His breath was not grassily gaseous as Desdemona had expected, but the stone-cool sweetness of petrichor. She leaned into the scent, sniffing appreciatively.

"Now," Farklewhit went on worriedly, "I don't have any flowers for you to hold—that's what you mortals do at weddings, isn't it?—but take this for proxy! It's colorful, anyway!" and thrust his corky quilted cap into her hand.

Desdemona grinned. "This'll do nicely, Nanny." She fluffed the sizzling pom-pom until it boi-yoi-yoinged in a spray of rainbow light.

Farklewhit gave an approving little hop and turned to the newly betrotheds, directing them to kneel in a row on the steps. He assigned the Gentry Sovereign center place. Susurra loudly objected to this—in a bossy voice that reminded Desdemona uncomfortably of herself—saying that, as Alban Idris was the tallest of them, it should at least kneel several steps below herself and Chaz. She did this, Desdemona suspected, mostly for Chaz's sake—as Susurra could dream herself any height she desired. They all adjusted accordingly.

A line of marble giants flanked the bottom of the dais, their backs to the ceremony, making certain the gentry did nothing to disrupt the proceedings. But nothing seemed unlikelier—the gentry were overjoyed! Wings fluttered, scales glistered, feathers puffed, tentacles slithered. The subjects of the Valwode crowded as close as they dared.

The ceremony began with a stomp of Farklewhit's cloven hoof. It rang out like a glass bell against the dais. A hush fell. Farklewhit stood center, obscured to the onlookers below by the rising beams of the Antler Crown, but from behind those tangled tines, his harsh and merry voice (like a donkey attempting to perform the rites of a priest) brayed up and out:

"Here is Alban Idris, enthroned sovereign of Dark

Breakers! Made by mortal hands, enkindled by gentry magic, it is Nyx the Nightwalker's Anointed Heir, faithful servant of the Valwode, who, having failed its directive to dream the Veil-Between-Worlds anew and eager to atone for its failure, makes reverence before you now."

The Antler Crown comprised eight branching beams growing in a circle from the Gentry Sovereign's skull, their highest points all entangled. Farklewhit's right hand reached out to grasp the beam at its left temple, his fingers closing around the base between brow tine and burr. At his touch, that beam's whole branch began to glow: not the soft, pervasive gloaming everywhere to be seen in Dark Breakers, but the dark, blood-fed ivory of living bone.

"Here is Susurra the Night Hag, Twelfth Daughter of Kalos Kantzaros! Princess of the Koboldkin, Erl-Daughter of Bana the Bone Kingdom, she is Nyx the Nightwalker's Appointed Heir and traitor to the Valwode, who, having served her sentence and paid off her debts to the Veil, makes reverence before you now."

When Farklewhit's left hand closed around the rightmost beam of the Antler Crown, that bone-colored branch also smoldered with an inward fire. But here he paused, and his thin black lips wobbled a bit. Alarmed, Desdemona reached out and squeezed his arm. He glanced over gratefully, his eyes tender and full of tears, then cleared his throat and boomed anew:

"Here is the Maiden Mallister, mortal-born! Beloved of Susurra and of Alban Idris, she is the chosen bride of both, who, having forsaken Athe to dwell apart from mortal kind and live with her beloveds in the Valwode, makes reverence before you now."

Though the courtroom of Dark Breakers was enclosed, with no visible windows or doors, a wind picked up. Perhaps it blew from Farklewhit himself, for his braying voice had become the sound of a cyclone, the thunder of hurricanes making landfall, the splitting of the earth along a fault line.

It was a voice Desdemona knew well. She had only heard it twice in her life, but if she grew old and bent and forgot all else, that voice would remain.

Before the gentry court, Farklewhit was changing. His fleece was peeling back, his limbs elongating. His horns were looping, leaping, lifting from his head with the fluidity of flame. His hands, grasping the Antler Crown, were no longer hard and brown and furred in fleece, but quicksilver and flaring white fire, with talons of smoldering emerald, filigreed in copper.

"I," said the Kobold King, "Kalos Kantzaros, declare these promised three to be wed hereafter. Let the scionhorn be sundered!"

With an energetic twist, his lightning-colored hands

wrenched upward and—CRACK!—ripped the two side beams of the Antler Crown from their seated pedicles in the Gentry Sovereign's skull.

Alban Idris made no sound, but its subjects sighed with a certain satisfaction. A few applauded. Someone struck up music—a melody like spiders playing their own webs. There was a great tinkling, and the sound of wings. A few gentry levitated several feet off the floor in elation. Even the stern policemen giants, whose backs were to the proceedings, softened with approval of their sovereign sibling.

Of the six remaining beams of the Antler Crown, two protruded from Alban Idris's wide forehead, four from the back of its head. Two bloody holes marred the marble-white curls just above its temples. Chaz looked horrified, and began to weep, and threw her arms about Alban Idris as if to protect it from further harm. Even Susurra seemed slightly concerned, stretching back her hand to touch its shoulder. Alban Idris smiled bravely at them, tears standing out in its black-flash eyes.

"Do not let the sight disquiet you. What is missing will grow back. We suffered worse hurt when first the Antler Crown sprang full-horned from our skull."

"Sovereigns!" the Kobold King remonstrated, and the three newlyweds snapped forward like scolded children to attend him. His focus burned upon them with the radiant precision of sunlight through diamond. Desdemona both wished and feared his attention would fall on her as well, bringing her to her knees as it had done in the World Beneath the World Beneath. She wanted to search out Farklewhit behind those acid-green eyes and see if she could pull him forth as from his own hat. But the Kobold King did not so much as flicker a glance her way.

"As the scionhorn is sundered," he announced, "let it now be grafted in good faith. You three," he said, "shall be Companions-at-Throne in the Valwode. *Teach each other to dream.*" And lifting the severed beams high, Kalos Kantzaros plunged them down again, driving them like stakes through the centers of Chaz's and Susurra's skulls.

The sound they made was neither gasp nor croak nor scream. There was no breath behind it, only the crunch-shock of impact. Desdemona screamed for them. She pounced forward, teeth bared, but the Gentry Sovereign lunged to stop her, dragging her to the steps and pressing her down.

"Be still!" it whispered. "All is well!"

Desdemona writhed, trying to get to Chaz.

Below the dais, the gentry court started dancing in a frenzy of celebration. The Bog Sisters whirled in a merry circle of linked arms. A creature with the head of a hare and the body of a young boy gamboled up to a great, burly, bearded man, whose beard was a waterfall of roses, to pluck handfuls of petals from his face and throw them into the air. They did not fall but took flight like butterflies, flitting through the crowd. No one seemed to notice, or noticing, care, about the blood fountaining from Chaz's skull, or the ichor from Susurra's, how they staggered and would have fallen, but that the Kobold King held them upright by the horns in their heads.

Susurra steadied first. Several segmented strands of her hair shook themselves out of their stupor, wavered upright, and whipped round the beam planted in her forehead, wrapping it blackly like trained ivy on a trellis. This, it seemed, was an act of integration, welcoming the antler into Susurra as part of her body. Within seconds, her beam took root and began to send out shoots. A circlet of smaller black horns budded from her head.

It went harder for Chaz. Her knees sagged. Her head lolled forward. Blood spurted from her skull, pulsing with each heartbeat, splashing up onto her antler until it was soaked: stem and branch and tine. Bright red fuzz began to velvet the antler, starting at the base, crawling to the tip. The longer Chaz bled, the more her antler was fed. The deeper the nap, the darker the velvet. Crimson. Carmine. Garnet. Burgundy. But she would not stop bleeding.

It seemed to Desdemona that all the blood in Chaz's body was erupting up through her skull. That she, being mortal, had sustained a mortal wound. When her heartbeat started to stagger, when the pause between spurts lengthened, only *then* did the antler finally take root. Eight pedicles sprouted all around Chaz's skull, pushing up through her soaked-dark hair, each new bud as wine-cherry-blood-berry-red as the original graft. But Chaz did not straighten. Her eyes did not open.

"Dream wild," said Kalos Kantzaros in final blessing. "Dream dangerous. Dream true."

His form became unfixed. Soon, he was only a corkscrewing column of quicksilver flame, turning, turning, swirling ceiling-ward. The column touched the high roof of the royal courtroom, where it flashed green and reversed direction, hurtling back into the ground like a mechanized earth auger. Where it disappeared.

"Chaz?" Desdemona screamed, clawing away from Alban Idris. "Chaz!"

The sounds of celebration and laughter drowned out her frantic cries.

Susurra—Antler Crown full-grown now, lacquer-black like her hair—held Chaz by one arm. Alban Idris held her other. They both leaned in to kiss her: forehead, eyelids, nose, the corners of her drained-pale mouth.

When they stepped back, only Desdemona was left gripping her about the waist, holding on like a drowning woman clings to flotsam, hoping it will carry her ashore.

And when Chaz opened her eyes, she was no longer human.

The blue of her irises floated like jewels on scarlet scleras. Her own Antler Crown bloomed and branched upon her brow, still covered in red velvet, but showing the first glimpses of the red iron underneath. She did not shake free of Desdemona but did not look to her either. Her strange regard met that of Susurra and Alban Idris. She smiled for them, her teeth the same red iron as her horns.

"Is it well, Consort?" Alban Idris asked her.

If Chaz's laughter sounded shaky, at least it was familiar to Desdemona. "It is well, Consort."

Susurra grinned then as only goblin girls and Gentry Queens can grin. She flourished like a statesman and cried, "Then, Consorts, let us feast! For tonight we dream in each other's arms—and wake to a Valwode born anew!"

14

QUEEN AT THE THRESHOLD

LATER, THEIR EXIT UNNOTICED in the jubilant midst
of the revelry, Desdemona and Chaz slipped away to
walk in the orchard. Branches glittered. Gold. Silver.
They flowered, bore fruit-like gems. Gem-like fruit. Desdemona snapped off the prettiest branches as she passed
under them, biting her tongue, which wanted to snap,
too. Make the break clean between them. Never mind the
bleeding. The leave-taking. She would not let it.

Smiling wryly, Chaz followed in the wake of her de-
molition, silently collecting fallen boughs and arranging
them in a bouquet of precious metals that sagged with
jewels. They wandered the Woodwyrm tunnel through
the thornwood, and when the flowers started singing at
them, Chaz spared them a single glare from her alluvial
larimar-on-scarlet eyes and said, "Hush."

The flowers furled back into chastened buds, practically vibrating with obedient silence.

"Sopranos," Chaz muttered when Desdemona raised

her eyebrows. "They'll eat you alive."

Desdemona's grin was a little lopsided. "They tried, last time I came through."

That seemed a hundred years ago now.

Chaz tugged one of her tails. The tail swatted back. "You've changed since then."

"Some. You too."

"Some."

Before Desdemona was ready for it, they came to the luminous cairn of the Mirradarra Doorway.

Chaz stopped. She handed Desdemona her armful of precious metals, tucking Farklewhit's hat into their midst like a yarn bomb in a jewelry box. "This isn't goodbye forever, Desi," she said. "So don't go off ruining lives and wrecking nations just because you're feeling sorry for yourself. I know you."

"But, Chaz, will I . . ." Desdemona hesitated. "Do you think . . . going home will change me . . . back?"

"If I returned," Chaz countered patiently, "would I change back?"

"No!" Desdemona burst out. "You were always *you*!"

Chaz spread her hands. Her bloodstained ivory gown sparkled like hellish stars. "And so," she said, "you will still be you, Tattercoats. Wherever you are. Whatever that looks like."

"But . . ."

Desperate for reassurance, Desdemona burst out, "*How* will I ever see you again? The Valwode won't mistake me for a poet without you. There's not enough champagne in Athe! I'll be stuck up there forever, kicking my Ernanda heels . . ."

Chaz shook her head, her crown of horns shedding flecks of velvet like drops of blood. "When the bone bells ring at midnight, the walls of Breaker House open, and we of the Valwode take what we want. That is how the stories go. Well. Now Breaker House will have something that *I* want. Be ready."

A sound inside the cairn interrupted them: the barking of dogs, echoing off the gray crystal walls of the grotto. Chaz turned toward the sound.

"The tithe returns."

Soon they came bursting out of the split in the gray crystal rock, dozens of goblin hounds, their coats sleeked down with river water like stained-glass windowpanes cast back into the forge: cadmium-yellow, verdigris, indigo, cranberry, cobalt, ruby, orange, and peacock-green. They circled Desdemona and Chaz, sniffing, exploring, and then, satisfied, sat back on their haunches in a silent crescent, watching them with human eyes.

Far away, on the other side of the thornwood, in the direction of Dark Breakers, Desdemona could hear the bone bells start to ring.

"It's midnight above," Chaz observed. "Quickly now. There's not much time."

"How do you know it's midnight?" Desdemona demanded.

Chaz flicked her Antler Crown. The red iron rang. "It's in me now, Desi. This dream of time. Come on—I'll open a door for you." Grabbing Desdemona's hand, she ducked inside the Mirradarra Doorway. But Chaz did not lead her to the river's edge, whose mouth emptied into the world below. Instead, she laid her freckled, blood-speckled hand against one of the rock walls and knocked three times—just like Farklewhit had done to the stalagmite in Breakers Beyond.

As it had done then, the rock shifted, the crystals parting like draperies to reveal a staircase winding up. These steps were made of hard, compact coal, such as might lead, eventually, to the shaft of a colliery.

"Go on, Desdemona," Chaz said. "Take them home."

15

REVERSE KATABASIS

CANDLETOWN COMPANY'S MERULA COLLIERY served the Grackle, Cowbird, and Bobolink Mines. Miles and miles of underground galleries interconnected these mines, with five pits of access, all sealed since the disaster.

Eventually, after another dizzying, thigh-burning, lung-wheezing, *eternal* climb—during which Desdemona contemplated eating her metal bouquet, Farklewhit's hat, the dogs, and herself—the anthracite stair leveled out into a tunnel shored up by wooden beams. Two rusted metal tracks led away from what became, as soon as it ceased being a stairway through worlds, a solid rock wall.

The moment her foot touched the metal rail, Desdemona's furs sagged off her skin. She tested her tails. Not a single wag. They hung limply off her belted coat, no longer a part of her. Salmon-gold ribbons of a ragged taffeta hem flapped around her ankles.

She was home.

Before she could wail at the loss, even the light from Farklewhit's hat winked out, taking her vision with it.

No night-sight now. Only darkness.

The air was close. This far underground, the climate was tropical but stuffy. The pack of hounds, however, seemed indifferent to air quality, their eager shapes trotting past her when she hesitated, their paws making no noise in the debris-filled tunnels. Trembling, sore, sweltering, Desdemona picked her way after them, following the rails by tentative touch, with only her breathing to bear her company, until, gradually, the silence began to murmur and seethe. Darkness split into dancing shadows. Somewhere nearby—just up ahead—there were lights. They were moving her way. No human voices yet reached her straining ears (she was, alas, down to a single, dull pair now), but the urgent activity of breath whistled down the shaft: the rhythmic, mechanical inhalations and exhalations of oxygen rebreathing apparatuses. And footsteps: plodding, diligent, deliberate.

The dogs had vanished around a bend. Desdemona hastily stopped on the tracks and drew back against a wall. Tucking the bouquet Chaz had given her under her arm, she shook out Farklewhit's cap and quickly flipped it inside out, jamming it over her head. She had seen him do this trick her first time at the Mirradarra Doorway to effect a quick disappearance and only hoped it would work for her. The last thing she wanted was to explain to a party of rescue workers how the socialite daughter of H.H. Mannering, Candletown Company heiress, the Anthracite Princess herself, came to be in the depths of Merula Colliery with the sole survivors of the underground explosion. Who just happened to be dogs. If they were still dogs.

The hat sort of melted around her face, stink-first, and Desdemona *felt* herself disappear. She leaned into that fetor-of-Farklewhit blackness, closing her eyes as a feeling of intense comfort washed over her. It wasn't the whole world going black, she knew—only herself in it—as if she and Farklewhit were alone together in Bana the Bone Kingdom on an errand of great importance, with only a pink apron between their nakedness. Feeling safer now, steadier, Desdemona plunged ahead around the bend—right into the milling midst of miners and rescue workers.

The latter were sometimes called "frogmen" because of their equipment, which was based on that of combat divers. In fact, the monstrous hodgepodge of their apparatuses lent them more a chimerical aspect than amphibious, with their pig-snouted rebreathers, the camel humps of their great backpacks, their rubber-skinned suits, and their goggle eyes. In contrast, the miners looked like they had stepped full-formed out of Merula's dusty womb.

They were tense and nervous, faces black with coal dust, eyes like carbide lamps. They said almost nothing but allowed themselves to be patched and palpitated, swabbed, and bandaged. The rescue workers, communicating mostly through hand gestures, offered them sandwiches.

Refusing the food, one of the miners said in a soft, crackly voice that he thought maybe they'd been eating all right, out of the lunch pails of their dead pals, but they'd drunk the last of their water last night and could use a swig?

The rescue workers' response was a swift deluge of canteens, then just as efficiently, they ushered the bewildered miners up the same shaft whence they had come. Invisible Desdemona slunk in their wake, one arm full of gold and silver branches, the other piled with the sandwiches the miners had let fall, all of which she single-mindedly consumed long before they reached the surface.

Then, sunlight—like a blow to the head.

The world became the negative of a photograph. White silhouettes against a black background. This impression faded slowly into color and substance, and soon the static roar of radio silence splintered into many noises all jabbering at once.

Desdemona shielded her eyes and humped up her stinking furs all about her for protection. She knew she was invisible, that she was safe from the pops and clicks of the cameras, the journalists yelling questions to the rescue team, the police whistles, the cries of bereaved friends and families converging on the survivors. Even so, she wished herself back in the mines. Better yet, in the labyrinthine midnight caverns two worlds below . . .

It took her a few more minutes of recalibration before she noticed the protestors marching around the colliery, their numbers swelling by the minute as word of the rescue spread throughout Seafall. There were strikers from different labor unions—the Mine Workers, the Iron Knights, the Leressan Teamsters, the United Locomotive Engineers. There was her former lover Salissay, side by side with Lu "The Pit Bull" Dimaguiba, Salissay's auntie and union steward to the ULE. She stood chatting with Mrs. Mannering and Mrs. Alderwood, who both wore very large hats and carried even larger signs that read: RETREAT LATER! RESCUE NOW!

Other fashionably dressed women, of the sort Chaz called "Tracy's hyenas," all wearing similar hats and carrying similar signs, faced off against the Candletown Company Coal Enforcers, H.H.'s private security squad, whose ranks were joined by the sheriff of Seafall's citizen posse. The deputies were armed with rifles, billy clubs, and riot shields. The female philanthropists had custom shoes and tailored suits and surnames of note, and if these were not enough—which was always a grim possibility—the heft of their hand-bags and the steel tips of their umbrellas gave warning that they were more than ready to hit back.

Usually such an astonishingly photogenic confrontation would attract the attention of the press. But today, nothing less exciting than a fusillade could drag their lenses away from the rescue team emerging from the pit-head, survivors in tow. The rescuers shouted for order, for space. The crowd ignored them, swamping the miners with blankets, lifting them in their arms, bearing them away to waiting ambulances.

Desdemona stumbled after, pausing only once when she passed Salissay in her signature black-and-white-checkered coat, scribbling furiously in her notebook while taking a headcount of the survivors.

"Twenty-one," she was shouting excitedly. "Twenty-one recovered! Does anyone know their names? *Their names*?"

The number disturbed Desdemona for some reason. She tried to think. It wasn't the *right* number. She was so tired she couldn't remember what the right number should be. The hulk of her furs weighed on her. The bulk of a dozen dry-scarfed sandwiches sat edgily in her belly. Her bare feet were blistered and cracked.

Pushing past her aunt Audrey, who had joined her

well-coiffed comrades in jeering at H.H.'s bullyboys, Desdemona clambered into the bed of one of the rescue trucks. She squeezed between a pile of body suits and a stack of oxygen tanks, settled back, and was asleep before the engine coughed to life.

16

SEVERING THE LINE

IN THE VESTIBULE OF Breaker House, Desdemona divested herself of her filthy furs and ruined evening gown, leaving them, along with her gold and silver bouquet, in a heap on the floor. They reappeared out of invisibility as soon as they broke contact with her body, jeweled fruit sparkling against the marble tiles. Desdemona stood in her slip, shivering, Farklewhit's friendly cap her only point of warmth.

She was glad to remain imperceptible—even if just to herself. She was not yet ready to espy her own reflection in some gilded mirror. This mortal body. This pared-down, plucked-raw flesh, nubbly, horripilating.

The floor was like ice underfoot. It was long past midnight, and the house was completely dark, shut up for the season now that H.H. was gone to the continent. But Desdemona could make her way through Breaker House blindfolded and drunk. Had, in fact—on more than one occasion. She padded from the vestibule into

H.H.'s library and pulled the chain of the green-shaded brass banker's lamp on the desk. Then she picked up the phone and called her mother.

"Hi, Tracy's place!" said a woman who was not Tracy.

"This is her daughter," said Desdemona. "Put her on, please."

"Oh, yeah, hey, Dolores! One sec! Tracy? Traaaaaaace!" the voice sang out. "Hey, were you at the protest today?" she asked Desdemona excitedly. "We had upward of fifty thousand marchers by the end! They kept trying to arrest us, but there aren't enough jails in Southern Leressa! Oh, here's Tracy! It's Dolores, Tracy."

"Who?" asked Tracy, laughing, and said into the mouthpiece, "Hello?"

"Hello, Mother."

Tracy's gasp almost sucked Desdemona ear-first through the phone lines. She said nothing for several seconds, then whispered very quietly, "Was that you? Did you bring them back?"

"Some," said Desdemona. "Not enough."

"It's never enough," Tracy said, still quietly. "But it's more than . . . more than nothing. It makes a difference. I promise."

"How many . . ." Desdemona trailed off. She knew the answer, but she wanted it verified.

"Salissay reported twenty-one recovered. We didn't

imagine—we couldn't believe—anyone had survived at all."

Desdemona shook her head. Kept shaking it. Twenty-one was wrong. It was *fifteen* short. Thirty-six. There were supposed to be *thirty-six*. A tithe was a tenth. Three hundred fifty-six had gone down that day. When was that? Three days ago? A week? A lifetime? And she had bargained to bring thirty-six back up.

She only realized she had bitten her tongue when she tasted blood.

"Mother." Desdemona turned her head, and spat on her father's desk, and did not wipe it away. "I need to know the combination to H.H.'s safe. There's something in it I need."

This time, Tracy did not hesitate at all.

"Do you have a pencil ready?"

~

The contract between the Mannerings of old and the Kobold King was written upon some manner of membranous vellum. No matter what Desdemona did to it—and she went after it like a mantis attacking a hummingbird—the material rejected all damage. It stretched like rubber. Objects rebounded from it. She sawed it with scissors, skewered it with letter openers, even tried running it through with a poker. To no avail. The contract was as impervious to outside attack as H.H. Mannering's reputation, which had weathered far worse than scandal with nothing but a smirk.

When destroying the thing didn't work, Desdemona decided to try reading it. Decorated drop caps initiated each paragraph, lettered in various colored inks. Glowing illustrations paraded through the marginalia. But no matter which angle she came at it, Desdemona could not decipher the writing itself; she suspected it was not in any language originating in Athe. But the illustrations were plain enough.

The top of the contract was a thing of turquoise skies and green grasses, with golden suns and stars spanning the uppermost margin. The bottommost margin swirled with midnight inks, and silvery, spider-haired creatures perched on clusters of jeweled outcroppings that jutted up from the lower edges of the page. A wisp of indigo-colored smoke unfurled across the middle of the page, representing the Veil-Between-Worlds, wherein vague forms of gentry creatures pranced and preened and gamboled. In the bottom left corner of the contract was a slender, smoky figure, crowned in green flame. One of its arms was lifted, fingers outspread, reaching up and to the right. A silver shackle looped its wrist, the silver chain welded to it winding all the way through the bewildering writing to attach to a second shackle at the top right corner, this one worn by a second figure, human, reaching down and to the left.

No doubt that dark, determined face belonged to some Mannering ancestor whose name had since been lost to history. But Desdemona could read the expression on it like it was her own face: stormy and stubborn and frightened. Whatever the document *said*, Desdemona knew what it *meant*. It was the details of that first tithe: the exchange of favors between worlds, drawn up for desperate reasons no one alive, human or goblin, now knew. Whatever its original purpose, the contract was now corrupted. H.H. and his forebears had turned the tithe into a blood-barter for power. Murder and disappearance in exchange for the stuff of the deep: metals, minerals, coal, oil.

Desdemona sighed. What did it matter *why* the Kobold King—or rather, his predecessor—had entered into this contract? Why should she care why he would want humans in his world?

But she did wonder: Was it for their company? For particular human skill sets that did not come easily to goblins? Or perhaps—as the Gentry Sovereign had told Chaz—for their *perspective*? Something to keep the worlds in balance . . . ?

Desdemona rapidly grew weary of this futile line of inquiry. Already the languid ease of her life in Athe was tugging at her, as deadly and as stultifying in its way as the singing flowers of the Valwode. She wasn't sure what she would become after a bath and a change of clothes, when the beautiful stench of her time below disintegrated under scented soap, talcum powder, a spritz of Aniqua Adrian perfume—and whether, at that point, she would even care anymore. She had no thought for the future; all she wanted was to destroy something *now*. Chaz would have understood her in this mood. Desdemona was not sure there was anyone left in her own world who did.

Finally, when all her initial attempts at annihilating the contract failed, Desdemona marched over to the fireplace, which was the largest in Breaker House. Tossing the contract into the impeccable hearth, she snatched a box of Albright Safety Matches ("Support Seafall Industries!") from the mantel, struck one to flame, and kneeling on the hearthrug, laid the lit match to one illuminated corner of the contract. A turquoise bonfire leapt up immediately, scarlet at the tips, and Desdemona shouted her triumph.

Then she shouted again, dismayed, as the flames ran off the parchment like water and died on the hearthstones. Hurling the matchbox against the wall, Desdemona roared, "I'll take an ax to you next!"

"Wouldn't work," said a voice from the fireplace. "There're specific rules to this sort of thing."

"Nanny!" Desdemona dropped to her hands and knees and crawled forward eagerly. She almost started laughing, babbling, begging to be taken back—but remembered just in time. "Or is it," she asked suspiciously, *"Your Dark Majesty?"*

The fireplace was more than large enough to contain the Umber Farklewhit, even when he was lounging at full stretch on his side, propped up on one elbow, hooves crossed. A muted thumping came from the hearthstones behind him, where his tail wagged against them. Desdemona wished she had a hundred tails to wag back.

"I'm only Kantzaros at need," Farklewhit replied nonchalantly. "When I call him, he takes over. Or he calls me, and I'm suddenly there, where he can't be. We are each other, yes—but we are also separate. And sometimes both at once. If you see what I mean?"

"I don't."

"Well . . ."

Farklewhit scratched. Scratched everywhere. Scratched indulgently, luxuriously, extravagantly. Desdemona started scratching herself out of sheer covetousness.

"So, see," he explained, "once upon a time, Kalos Kantzaros had twelve daughters. By and by he decided—preoccupied with responsibilities as he was, and not being, exactly, you know, what you might call *cuddly*—that a nursemaid was in order. So he made me from himself, and set me apart from himself, bounding me in nursery walls with a list of constraints and duties, and left me in care of our girls. After that, he went about his business, and forgot, mostly, what he had done. I didn't mind. I had more than plenty to occupy me. But one by one, our girls grew tall. One by one, they went off on their adventures, and I was abandoned to my own devices. I grew strong in myself—separate from the self who made me. But not exactly all the way."

"How does that even work?" Desdemona asked dubiously.

Farklewhit stopped scratching to think. "You humans have two brains, right? One in your head, one in your stomach?"

She nodded uncertainly. She remembered learning something along those lines in uni: how the stomach has its own ganglion, sort of a pre-brain—a thinking unit, separate from the brain seated inside the skull.

"And your little brain, your stomach brain, that's what you call your gut instinct, right?" Farklewhit asked.

Desdemona nodded again.

"Well, me? I'm like the Kobold King's stomach brain, housed in this Farklewhit you see before you. My thoughts may not be *his*, but they influence him nonetheless."

"And you speak with his voice," said Desdemona, rec-ollecting Susurra mentioning something of the sort just before the wedding.

Farklewhit admitted, bashfully, "Sometimes. Though it's a bit like burping acid! I'm so scalded after, so stretched and furiously formless, that I have to dive down-world to cool off. But I'm back now, with a change of apron and a shine on my hooves—here for all your Farklewhit concerns!"

He stroked the contract he was currently half reclining on and offered up another of his winsome grins.

"Now, Tattercoats, trust me, I'm awfully good at goblin contracts . . ."

Desdemona thumped back on her heels. "Trust you? You bamboozled me once already!"

Farklewhit looked shocked. And shifty.

"I, bamboozle? Tattercoats, you wound me!"

"My exchange with Kalos Kantzaros," Desdemona spat, "was for *thirty-six* men. Thirty-six miners! How many came out with me?" she asked, then bellowed, "Twenty-one!" and slapped the hearthstones with the flat of her hand. "Twenty-one, Nanny! Where are my other fifteen?"

Farklewhit nervously tugged at his curly horns. "Oh, Tattercoats! It's not so *simple*. Yes, we bargained. Yes, you fulfilled your end—*beautifully*, may I add," he said with an admiring flutter of his eyelashes. "But every tithe who comes down to Breakers Beyond is offered full citizenship of Bana. Difficult as it may be for you to believe, there were a few miners who preferred going native, as it were, to going back to work for your father."

Desdemona slumped and almost fell. Without her tails, she felt hideously unbalanced.

"You still owe me fifteen lives."

"I? Do *I* owe you? Or does Kalos Kantzaros?"

"You, him, either, both." Desdemona rallied, declaring, "Nanny, I want my fifteen lives!"

"And you'd, what," Farklewhit challenged her dryly, "pluck a goblin subject from Bana like the fruit of an Ympsie tree and drag them, unwilling, up-world to make them live again in the light?"

"I'd ask them first!"

"You bargained for *miners*."

"Yes, and you shortchanged me!"

Instead of exploding back at her, like her father would have done, Farklewhit paused and then asked mildly, "Well, Tattercoats, what do you propose we do about that?"

She blew out a breath, glaring at the contract, which had started to roll itself up again like an infernal fern.

"Does that thing burn, Nanny?"

"Not in this fire or the next."

"Would you burn it if you could?"

"Oh," Farklewhit breathed out, "I'd extinguish myself and Kalos, too, if doing so would destroy it."

"What can?"

"Only a Mannering," Farklewhit said.

Desdemona caught her breath.

"Or rather . . ." He cleared his throat. "Or rather, only the end of the Mannering line."

Her mouth fell open as she absorbed the implications of this. Farklewhit quickly wagged his head at her; Desdemona could not tell if he was nodding or shaking it.

"Not your *death*, Tattercoats. Well, not necessarily. After all, your father might produce again."

"No-o," Desdemona said slowly. "Mother tried for years to get me. H.H. has been with the Countess even longer—she was much younger than Mother when she met my father—and they've tried, too. It was"—her teeth clenched briefly—"made *plain* to me, on several *memorable* occasions, that if Lupe ever spawned, H.H. would straightaway legitimize her whelp and disown me, bilking me of my inheritance." She tapped her knee with a grubby fingernail, missing her claws. "You can imagine how eager that made me to slip monk's pepper into his coffee each morning. Not that I ever did."

"But you thought about it."

"Yes."

"More than once."

"Yes."

Desdemona snuck a glance at him. Farklewhit was grinning broadly, exposing all of his square yellow teeth.

"You are such a goblin girl!" he exclaimed. "How you ended up in a mortal uterus is beyond my comprehension. You did *very well* as a Thousandfurs, you know. Dear Tattercoats..." He trailed off invitingly. His slit-pupil gaze grew very compelling.

Desdemona looked down at her lap, full of longing and abashed by it. Inhaling deeply, she was rewarded by a dizzying stink—though her present nose lacked the ability to detect the piquant complexity of the bouquet. In that moment, she decided she would not stand for it anymore. She wanted her sense of smell *back*.

Slapping her palm on the hearthstones again, Desdemona flattened one corner of the contract and blew out all her breath on a sharp "Ha!" like she was kicking a horse to gallop. "A bargain, Ambassador Farklewhit!"

"I am ready."

And he was. Suddenly Farklewhit was squatting on his glossy black hooves, one hand pressing over hers where it lay upon the contract. They were almost nose-to-nose.

Desdemona held his gaze. "Do you speak for Kalos Kantzaros in this?"

"Tattercoats." Farklewhit's yellow eyes filled with

green flames, his horns shining like quicksilver. "I *am* he—voice and all. Even when—or especially when—he is not *paying attention*. Speak your words."

In a ringing voice, Desdemona proclaimed, "I, the last of my line, will revoke the name Mannering in return for the name Tattercoats. I will break the alliance between my family and yours, renounce Athe, and live all my days—all my *nights*, I mean—in the World Beneath the World Beneath. But"—her voice dropped—"I want full citizenship in Bana. And I want the fifteen lives, Your Majesty, that are *owed* me. Perhaps there are others who are trapped beneath, who want a way out but cannot find it. I will be their doorway into daylight. *And you will not stop me.*"

Beneath their hands, Desdemona felt the lettering on the contract shift and writhe. The pictures began redrawing themselves. Colors and gilding seeped up and bled around their fingers. But negotiations were not finished. The contract was an agreement between two worlds, not one.

They were forehead-to-forehead now, Farklewhit and Desdemona. The sharps of his horns brushed the outer edges of her ears. His musk mingled with her unwashed odor, and she inhaled this new fragrance raptly through her nose.

In his bottomless Kalos Kantzaros boom, Farklewhit

countered: "If you would be Tattercoats full through, a true goblin of Bana, you will be charged with a vocation. You must—and shall!—*serve*. Begin as my courier, my messenger between worlds. You shall forthwith be granted the ability to slip your thousand furs and slide back into them at will. We shall put your knightly knack for rescuing to good use."

When he bopped her nose with his, he was Farklewhit again.

"Now, isn't *that* a nobler way of saying 'you shall fetch and carry on my whim'? Anyway, it's not like we'll ask you to steal *babies* for the glory of the Bone Kingdom. I've had my fill of diapers, thank you. But by trick, temptation, or trade, we must cross-pollinate the three petals of the World Flower—lest all our peoples dwindle and diminish. It was always our way to take in the unwanted of other worlds, even after our borders were mostly sealed. We just hate it"—Farklewhit glared at the oil painting of H.H. Mannering that was mounted on the wall opposite the fireplace—"when we're *forced*."

Something like butterflies, but with more claws and incandescence, swarmed Desdemona's chest cavity. "So," she reiterated, "as long as a mortal is *willing* to come beneath, I can escort them down-world?"

Farklewhit made that indeterminate wagging motion of his head. "Well... not without *consulting* me at least—or we'll be flooded with doughty journalists and pesky sopranos!" He winked.

The writing kept on scribbling and re-scribbling itself beneath their palms, but Desdemona knew it the moment the contract settled into its new shape. She stared thoughtfully at her hand, now joined with Farklewhit's, where it rested on the vellum. Around their fingers, the marginalia of the contract had filled in with new faces. Some of them she recognized. She had once feared the sight of them, had been filled with sickness and disgust and pity, and loathed them because of that. Now she could only marvel at their potential.

Oh, no. It was not *opera singers* she would be bringing to Breakers Beyond on her first journey home.

"After all," Desdemona said slowly, her forehead still pressed to Farklewhit's, "there's *stealing* . . . and then there's—more like Chaz in the Valwode, right?—there's . . . inviting? A kind of immigration?"

She felt Farklewhit's smile curl around hers. "Precisely."

17

MEND HER WITH RUBIES

THE GOBLIN KNOWN AS Tattercoats Thousandfurs looked almost exactly like Desdemona Mannering. Except, beneath her sleek brown walking suit with its tessellated puppytooth pattern, she had tucked her nine tails, which made wearing a bustle absolutely redundant. The velvet applejack hat pulled low over her brow hid *all* her ears. Smoky quartz lenses concealed her light-sensitive eyes. From a fob at her waistcoat hung a pocket watch that, when opened, showed the glowing rune of an hourglass. Her time outside Bana was strictly limited.

Tattercoats approached a nurse at the receptionist station at the Seafall City Working Women's Almshouse. She kept her smile small, careful not to flash her tiny sharp teeth.

"Hello. I have an appointment in the Matchbox."

The nurse looked taken aback at this breezy reference to the ward in question. But no one who worked in that building would dare castigate a Mannering. The nurse gestured to a row of chairs and invited, "Have a seat, Miss Mannering. I'll fetch someone to escort you up."

The Seafall City Working Women's Almshouse was an institution for the ailing poor of the working class, who, unable to keep their jobs due to their conditions, could not afford medical attention. It consisted of four six-bed wards, each nicknamed by the graveyard nurses in their gallows weariness: the "Undark Ward," where girls from the radium factory went to die; the "Stone Ward," where foundry workers, their lungs scarred to flint-like hardness after years spent inhaling particulate, struggled for breath; the "Printing Press," where women in different lead industries lay in seizures and poisoned comas; and finally the "Matchbox," where the Phossy Jaw Girls, their bones necrotizing from close contact with the white phosphorous used in matchmaking, disintegrated to death.

Work on the expansion of the Matchbox, funded by Mrs. Tracy Mannering's charity, had already begun. What had been the eastern wall of the reception room was now sealed off with tarp. Signage warned visitors that what lay beyond was a construction zone and to PLEASE FORGIVE OUR DUST. Instead of taking a seat, Tattercoats, loose-hipped and swaggering, ambled over near the site. She examined a scale model of the plans set up on a table. Next to it, a detailed sandwich board explained the project, complete with a pasted-on clipping from a recent article by Salissay Dimaguiba. The headline read: *TRACY'S PLACE: A HEROIC RENOVATION.*

Dimaguiba opened with the history of the Almshouse, which had been founded a hundred years ago by Lataisha Mannering and kept solvent by Mannering women ever since. She went on to give details about the new ward: designed especially for "the women who give their lives for light," it would be "outfitted with the very latest in medical technology" and staffed "by the first generation of female physicians allowed to graduate from the University of Southern Leressa."

Tattercoats could always tell when Salissay was planting the seeds of another feature article in whatever she was currently working on. Grinning, she kept reading.

The rest of the article was an interview with Tracy Mannering, mostly about the benefit she had staged for the new ward at the Seafall City Opera House. It ended with a description of Tracy, "staring into the middle distance," murmuring that her fondest hope was that "this ward will be my cenotaph" and that it would last "long after I am gone." In typical Dimaguiba style, the journalist concluded: "While it is to be hoped that Mrs. Mannering's work with the Southern Leressa Convention Respecting the Prohibition of White Phosphorous in Matches might one day bear *legislative* fruit, her new ward must serve as a reminder that any laws we propose to protect our factory workers will be passed far too late to save the patients admitted herein—both now and in the foreseeable future."

Tattercoats shook her head in undisguised appreciation, saluting the sandwich board with a gloved hand (the brown chamois disguising hard black claws and padded fingers) before moving on to examine the easel standing next to it. It was set up like a miniature shrine, with a row of plain glass devotional candles burning beneath it on a low wooden stool, along with a large lockbox that had a slot on top for donations. Upon the easel was propped a framed portrait of Mrs. Tracy Mannering, rendered in glowing pastels.

Elliot Howell's work, of course—Tattercoats could tell by his distinctive style, his explosive Voluptuist colors. In the portrait, Tracy sat enthroned upon a massive oak chair. She was dressed in red, the sash across her chest reading STRIKE THE MATCH! One arm was propped on the armrest. Her other hand was upraised, fingers pinched around a lit match. She held it close to her face, which was turned toward the flare in sober contemplation. The match illumined only half her features. The shadowed half suggested a skull—a typically Howellian reference to Last Century artists' obsession with memento mori.

Tattercoats stared at the portrait for many a long minute.

Then she blinked two pairs of eyelids and took a step back. Reaching into her brown leather attaché case, she removed a bouquet of gold and silver branches, whose long stems bowed with sparkling fruit-shaped gems, and stuffed the whole thing pell-mell into the donation box.

"Goodbye, Mother," whispered Tattercoats. "Good luck."

Behind her, the receptionist called out, "Miss Mannering? The Nurse Director will see you now."

~

The hour was late, and in the Matchbox, all the patients were asleep.

Tattercoats took a seat on a chair nearest the first cot. She adjusted her tails beneath her, opening her attaché case and rummaging within, not taking any particular care to be quiet. Seconds later, aware that the girl in the cot had awoken and was watching her, Tattercoats glanced up and grinned.

The girl stared up from her pillow with feverish solemnity. Early twenties. Lank hair. Barely any face left at all, the hole in her skin and muscle emitting an oily-sweet smell that Tattercoats could remember once finding revolting. Not any longer. She merely removed her applejack hat, letting all her ears spring loose, and the goblin beneath her skin rippled, revealing the patchwork of otter-mink-weasel-badger-bear-swan-ostrich-chinchilla-rabbit-squirrel-lynx-wolf-fox-what have you.

Leaning in close, Tattercoats whispered, "Do you know about the World Flower?"

A light dawned in the girl's laudanum-dulled eyes—Tattercoats took that flicker as good enough for a nod. She wasted no time, sliding to her knees beside the cot and drawing the contract from her attaché case, where she held it up like a children's book.

"I am charged to bring mortals into the Bone Kingdom. Anyone I like. Anyone who is worthy. Like the women in these illustrations, see?"

The marginalia of the contract was crowded with human figures undergoing goblin transformation as they descended to Bana. Those nearest the top were thin and sallow-faced, with awful abscesses eating their lower jaws and steel braces bearing them upright. But their counterparts, having passed into the lower half of the contract, into the night-dark ink and the green glow cast by the Kobold King's crown, were different. They had become creatures of the underground, part flesh, part gemstone. Their jaws were no longer gaping wounds but carved of ruby, white jade, sapphire.

One girl, her face identical to that of the girl on the cot, had a new jaw entirely carved of shining alabaster, with mother-of-pearl insets. Her teeth were gemstones. Her hair ran with living veins of copper and gold, and her bones were as strong as the iron crystal core of Athe.

"I know you're afraid," Tattercoats told the girl on the cot, holding her wide-eyed gaze all the while. "I know you're in pain. I want to help you. If what you see in the picture is what you wish to be—blink thrice, and I will make it so."

The girl did not blink, but her glance shifted slightly. Tattercoats followed her gaze to the other cots.

"I'll come for them, too," she promised. "I'll take as many as I can. You can help. Together, we'll empty the wards—Matchbox, Printing Press, Undark, Stone. We'll turn all these walls into doors."

That seemed to satisfy her. Dragging her gaze from the cots to the contract, the girl blinked once.

The illuminated vellum began to gleam like quicksilver.

She blinked twice.

Across the page, the words of the contract scrambled themselves, re-forming into the shape of a spiral staircase that wound down from the top edge of the contract to the bottom.

The girl blinked a third time.

Tattercoats cast the contract to the floor, where it unrolled into a trapdoor, which opened. The first slick mercury steps appeared in the next moment, and a moment later, there were a thousand more, going ever down, vanishing into the darkness.

"Take my hand," said the goblin Tattercoats. "It's beautiful, beneath."

Acknowledgments

I met my writing mentor Gene Wolfe when I was eighteen. Over years of brunches, conventions, road trips, and letters, the spirit of mimetic desire filled me; I grew to want two things desperately in order to be more like Gene. I wanted a World Fantasy Award (he had lots of those hanging around his shelves), and I wanted a Tor publication (likewise). When I had these things, I figured—at last!—I would have "made it." This novella completes the set. Now all I have to do is actually be more like him: as generous, as insightful, as brilliant. Thank you, Gene.

The stories set in the Dark Breakers world began with my admiration for author Sharon Shinn. I wanted to pen fantastical romances set in a semi-historical, artsy-fartsy, sort of scapigliatura-meets-hobgoblin milieu. Two of these novellas I self-published for fun and experimental purposes. Sharon loved both of them—and her love went a long way in urging me to finish *Desdemona*. Thank you, Sharon! And thank you, all you early readers of those first Dark Breakers books!

Which brings me to Rich Horton. Thank you, Rich

(whose name is synonymous with "champion" in my heart) for taking those first novellas seriously.

I was writing *Desdemona* from the end of 2016 to the end of 2017. "Times being what they are / dark and getting darker all the time" (Anaïs Mitchell, *Hadestown*), I found writing that year to be grindingly difficult. It was hard to feel like anything mattered, least of all art. But I have always loved reading my work aloud, and author Caitlyn Paxson was there through it all, listening to bits on the phone, reading her own work-in-progress in return, and encouraging, encouraging, encouraging. Thank you, Caitlyn.

And thank you, Sita, for listening—in the garden, in the bathtub, doing dishes, first thing in the morning or last thing at night whenever I called you up from two time zones away. You somehow always have time for me, Mama—and an exceptional ear.

Thank you to my editor, Ellen Datlow. What an abiding pleasure to work with you! And thank you, Markus Hoffmann, my agent at Regal Hoffmann & Associates. (I don't quite believe you are actually from this world. Maybe one world down? Or perhaps the World Beneath the World Beneath . . . ?)

To my Goblin Girls, my Infernal Harpies, my RAMP writing group, my Chicago cronies, and my Women of Westerly: I love you so much, and owe you the good cheer and gumption in me. Patty Templeton, Amal El-Mohtar, Nicole Kornher-Stace, Jessica Paige Wick, Betsie Withey, Christa Carmen, Ysabeau Wilce, Tiffany Trent, Ellen Kushner, Delia Sherman, Joel Derfner, Liz Duffy Adams, John O'Neill, Tina Jens, Jeanine Marie Vaughn, Rebecca Huston, Katie Redding, and Stephanie Shaw. Thank you, beloveds.

Thank you, Mir and Kiri, longest-running friends in existence. Thank you, Francesca Forrest and Tina Connolly and Robert V. S. Reddick for reading *Desdemona* upon its early completion and believing in me—you put the "courage" in encouraging.

You will see that this book is dedicated to Julia Rios, Moss Collum, and their black cat Desdemona, who has now gone down to dwell among the goblins. Julia and Moss know why, but I just wanted to thank them again. For everything. For being family.

And Carlos. Carlos Hernandez, companion of my life, writing partner, who stretched the nature of Farklewhit to encompass a Kobold King. To Carlos, my darling, my fiend, mi enjambre, mi esposo. You extraordinary beast. You beautiful human. Thank you. Thank you for relentlessly transforming the darkness of our times into the deep radiance of creation. "The arc of the moral universe is long," you remind me in my bleaker moments, "but it bends toward justice."

That quote, while extremely heartening, does come with a complex pedigree and context. Without the work of activists and human rights organizations like the ACLU, Amnesty International, Habitat for Humanity, Doctors Without Borders &c, along with millions of individual people, I do not think the arc of the moral universe would bend toward justice. So this book is for them, too. Thank you, thank you, thank you.

About the Author

C. S. E. COONEY lives and writes in the borough of Queens, whose borders are water. She is an audiobook narrator, the singer/songwriter Brimstone Rhine, and the author of the World Fantasy Award–winning *Bone Swans: Stories*. Her short fiction can be found in Ellen Datlow's *Mad Hatters and March Hares: All-New Stories from the World of Lewis Carroll's Alice in Wonderland*, Jonathan Strahan's *Best Science Fiction and Fantasy of the Year Volume 12*, Paula Guran's *2016 The Year's Best Science Fiction & Fantasy Novellas*, five editions of Rich Horton's *Year's Best Science Fiction and Fantasy*, Mike Allen's *Clockwork Phoenix Anthology* (3 and 5), *Lightspeed*, *Strange Horizons*, *Apex*, *Uncanny*, *Black Gate*, Papaveria Press, *GigaNotoSaurus*, *The Mammoth Book of Steampunk*, and elsewhere.

TOR·COM

Science fiction. Fantasy. The universe.

And related subjects.

*

More than just a publisher's website, *Tor.com* is a venue for **original fiction, comics,** and **discussion** of the entire field of SF and fantasy, in all media and from all sources. Visit our site today—and join the conversation yourself.

11/29/19 - 1/8/20